THE CAGE

Praise for *Mister Pip*

'As compelling as a fairytale—beautiful, shocking
and profound.' HELEN GARNER

'It reads like the effortless soar and dip of a grand piece of music,
thrilling singular voices, the darker, moving chorus, the blend
of the light and shade, the thread of grief urgent in every beat
and the occasional faint, lingering note of hope.' *Age*

'*Mister Pip* is a rare, original and truly beautiful novel.
It reminds us that every act of reading and telling is a
transformation, and that stories, even painful ones, may
carry possibilities of redemption. An unforgettable novel,
moving and deeply compelling.' GAIL JONES

'Poetic, heartbreaking, surprising…Storytelling, imagination,
courage, beauty, memories and sudden violence are the main
elements of this extraordinary book.' ISABEL ALLENDE

'A brilliant narrative performance.' *Listener*

'A small masterpiece…Lloyd Jones is one of the best
writers in New Zealand today. With the beautiful spare,
lyrical quality that characterises his writing, Jones makes
us think about the power and the magic of storytelling,
the possibilities—and the dangers—of escaping to the
world within.' *Dominion Post*

'A little Gauguin, a bit of *Lord Jim*, the novel's lyricism evokes
great beauty and great pain.' *Kirkus Reviews*

'Rarely, though, can any novel have combined charm, horror
and uplift in quite such superabundance.' *Independent*

'Lloyd Jones brings to life the transformative power of fiction…
This is a beautiful book. It is tender, multi-layered
and redemptive.' *Sunday Times*

Praise for *Hand Me Down World*

'We surely have sufficient evidence to trumpet Lloyd Jones as one of the most significant novelists writing today.' *Sunday Times*

'A masterful, prismatic piece of storytelling.' *Independent*

'An extraordinary novel...Jones is a daring writer who can be relied on to ignore expectation, and is becoming one of the most interesting, honest and thought-provoking novelists working today.' *Guardian*

'Delicate and beguiling. It spirits the reader into a world that is both fascinating and perplexing. Its charms are hard to resist; its questions are hard to avoid... a book of great mind and heart.' *Age*

'Jones's touch is deft yet bold...fine, demanding and morally acute.' *Sydney Morning Herald*

'Jones slowly reveals the secrets of Ines's story and its emotional momentum sweeps us up and makes us fellow travellers.' *Weekend Australian*

'A fine and moving story with enormous compassion, emotional depth and tender insight into humanity... a superbly written meditation on how the disenfranchised accept the world as it is handed to them, on the weakness of men, on the deeply moving kindness of strangers, and on the power of maternal love. It is a beautiful book.' *Sunday Mail*

'This is a writer who knows how to tell a story, deftly, surprisingly, magnificently.' *Weekend Herald* NZ

'As complex and as beautifully crafted as a fine patchwork quilt.' *South Taranaki Star*

'Haunting to the very final line.' *Daily Telegraph*

Lloyd Jones was born in New Zealand in 1955. His best-known works include *Mister Pip*, winner of the Commonwealth Writers' Prize and shortlisted for the Man Booker Prize, *The Book of Fame*, winner of numerous literary awards, *Hand Me Down World* and his acclaimed memoir *A History of Silence*. He lives in Wellington.

LLOYD JONES
THE CAGE

TEXT PUBLISHING MELBOURNE AUSTRALIA

textpublishing.com.au

The Text Publishing Company
Swann House
22 William Street
Melbourne Victoria 3000
Australia

First published in Australia by The Text Publishing Company, 2018.

Cover art and design by W. H. Chong.
Page design by Imogen Stubbs.
Typeset by J&M Typesetters.

Printed and bound in Australia by Griffin Press, an Accredited ISO AS/NZS 14001:2004 Environmental Management System printer.

ISBN: 9781925603224 (paperback)
ISBN: 9781925626278 (ebook)

A catalogue record for this book is available from the National Library of Australia.

This book is printed on paper certified against the Forest Stewardship Council® Standards. Griffin Press holds FSC chain-of-custody certification SGS-COC-005088. FSC promotes environmentally responsible, socially beneficial and economically viable management of the world's forests.

In memory of the late Michael Gifkins—
friend, and literary agent

1

Viktor is sick. It means this morning I have to do the feeding out. First, I chop some kindling for the woodburner in the dining room and take it up the stairs with the basket of wood. The air in the dining room still smells of last night. Roast chicken, laughter. A few table tops need to be wiped.

In the kitchen I boil the eggs, switch on the urn. The kitchen is uncomfortably shiny at this hour. My reflection too blurry to see myself properly.

I put the eggs and cups on a tray. In one of the guestrooms a shower is running. A toilet flushes. The door closes behind me. And I head back down the stairs. The door at the end has a pane of frosted glass that doesn't let in the light. With one hand I pull the door open, I have to hold it in place with my foot. Then the backyard rushes at me. The high brick wall that blocks the view of the neighbours. The broken garden swing under the oak, with only half a wish to be noticed. The small lawn with the stone rabbit—its ears pointing up, its eyes still, stalked by a threat that never retreats or gets any closer. A car accelerates up the street and the silence of a town still asleep returns.

More light pushes in from the countryside. Iron rooftops

crack and flare. In the sky the last of the night turns to morning and birds beat their wings as if suddenly touched.

Near the cage, a slept-in, faecal air. It is hard to take at this hour.

Doctor crouches in front of the feeding hole, scratching above his right ear. His fingers are filthy.

When their faces press up to the mesh there is no push or shove. Doctor opens his mouth wide for me to spoon in some boiled egg. It's a small thing, to spoon egg into the mouth of another, but it never fails to encourage tenderness.

Are the eggs okay?

Doctor nods.

The younger stranger remains on his hands and knees, his mouth still open. He wants toast, but I am not ready.

I want to concentrate on Doctor. Although I wish his eyes weren't so fearful.

Not too runny, are they? The eggs, I mean.

His eyes drop, and he mumbles and nods.

No butter on Doctor's toast. I remember that, and he nods appreciatively. The younger one likes his buttered.

I have to say—the smell of human shit is unpleasant at this hour. When it's my turn to feed out I will usually wait until I know they have finished.

The younger one is reliable, like clockwork. Doctor, less so.

They have a short-handled spade and plenty of soil to cover over their mess. But when I turn up with their eggs and toast, I can't help myself, my eye wanders across to the chewed-up corner of the cage.

What else? They take their tea differently. Doctor prefers black. The younger one, milk, two sugars.

2

When I suggest that he might consider cutting back on the sugar he reacts with mild surprise. My concern comes from a place inside of me that he cannot see. Less sugar? Does that mean I might be counted on in a different way? The calculation is pressed into the flesh around his eyes.

At dark, the strangers are at last returned to themselves. There is no one around to gape at them.

But, if I stand on the lid of the toilet on the first-floor landing of the hotel, I can see into their cage in the backyard. There is plenty of light from the hotel windows above.

Tonight, the younger one is doing press-ups. He never does that during the day. Sit-ups. Press-ups.

Doctor stares into the palm of his hand. Is it a watch? No. That's not right. I can see now. He is counting on his fingers— the days they have spent in the cage. One by one, the lights in the hotel rooms switch off for the night, and I climb off the toilet seat and head down to my room.

In the morning, as they evacuate their bowels, they stare up at the hotel windows with hurt eyes. Yes. With hurt eyes. I think that's right.

Is there anything new to report? ask the Trustees.

The press-ups and sits-ups are of interest.

Are they reason for concern?

I expect they are old behaviours. A source of comfort.

To address anxiety?

Who can say?

So far, the strangers have been uncooperative. They refuse to tell us anything useful about themselves.

3

They will acknowledge certain truths because it would be silly of them not to.

They were obviously on their way to somewhere. But where—they cannot say. They speak of a place that could be out of a storybook—a hearth, a fire in the grate, small children at play, food in plentiful supply.

We hardly know what to make of them. They look the same as us and, as far as we have been able to tell, display all the usual desires and appetites.

Yet they refuse to say where they are from. They say it over and over, a thousand times a day—they have no home. Imagine tortoises insisting they have no shells. Everyone is born to a place on this earth. And everyone has a cover they can slip in and out of.

We ask, we prod. They shake their heads, then look disconsolate.

What are they to do?

What are we to do?

We named the older one 'Doctor' after he helped a young mother whose toddler was sick. I was feeding out when the 'older one', as we knew him then, recommended lemonade to settle the child's stomach.

He's been called Doctor ever since.

The power of suggestion cannot be denied. His thick-set legs rise to meet the weight descending from his shoulders. Some gravitas gathers around his middle. His eyebrows are bushy and grey. His eyes are steady. They wish to know more.

The younger one is more of a mystery. He is less liked, but no one can say why. At morning tea, we try out different names for him. None will stick. It is as futile as looking for another name for an elephant or an antelope. Still, the name 'stranger' offers little purchase. It is like trying to hear water. You hear only what water flows against.

Several of the Trustees have asked, can we not do better? Is there something in the younger one's behaviour that distinguishes him? Or perhaps a physical feature?

At feeding out I examined him closely. The two-tone effect of his dirty hands often surprises me. I have just settled into the idea of him as filthy and he turns his hands over to reveal clean white palms. When he caught me looking he hid his hands in the pockets of his jacket. And as he turned away, the bright morning sun struck the cage and exposed a blemish to one side of his nose that I hadn't noticed before, probably on account of the grime and weathered condition of the skin.

I recommended to the Trustees that henceforth the younger one be known as Mole.

The next morning, there is some snuffling, now a snort. I've only ever seen Mole spit. So that will be him. Yes. I think so. The muttering? That's Doctor. I have a feeling the one he seeks is not in the cage.

A shift of limbs, now a bigger stir of body and interest. Doctor's eyes drop to the tray, and the corners of his mouth tighten.

I place the tray on the grass outside the cage. Then I take a knife and lop off the top of a boiled egg.

Salt?

A nod.

Pepper?

Another nod. These small courtesies surprise some of the Trustees. But, it is important that we continue to find ways to engage.

I dig the teaspoon in the egg, and reach through the feeding hole.

The egg is hot and Doctor has to juggle it to the back of his mouth, now to the front. He huffs and his eyes water. His mouth falls open. Flecks of egg white, crumbling bits of yellow stuck to his teeth.

He looks down at the tray to see what else there is.

Toast. Honey. The tea is still brewing in the pot.

Now Mole nudges Doctor away from the feeding hole. He pushes his hand through. He wants to feed himself.

There are rules about feeding out. I am not to hand the strangers any knives, forks, spoons or utensils which might be used against themselves or, God forbid, a hotel guest. For the same reason the strangers are asked to present their mouths to the hole. In a moment of anger or frustration, a hand may close into a fist, and we are determined to avoid any unpleasantness of that kind.

I crack the top off a second egg, place it and the teaspoon in the feeding hole, but Mole's interest has soured. He nods at the toast on the tray.

Do you want honey?

I have to repeat the question, until he mutters 'honey'.

I'm spreading the toast when Doctor pushes up against the cage with his urgent face.

Please, he says. Has there been any news?

No. There is no news.

But soon?

6

Yes. That is everyone's hope.

The woman from the agency? We were expecting a visit by now.

2

It is such a lovely morning. Summer is dragging on which is something the strangers should be grateful for. Mole is shitting at the rear of the cage where the soil is well dug over. Doctor spreads himself against the inside wall to obscure public view. It is a technique they learned in their first days in the cage. Doctor raises his arms and hands against the cage mesh, a gesture that never fails to irritate. Since what he really wishes to say is, *Look at me. Look at our situation!*

His voice of late hardly rises above a crusty whisper.

Last night, he says, there was music.

Yes. I was practising my clarinet.

His grey eyes close around the memory of what he heard.

I found it quite beautiful, he says.

He pushes himself back from the mesh and points towards the ground-floor window.

From over there, he says. That's where I thought I heard it.

Yes. That's where I practise.

I don't mention that it is also where I live and that the window is one of two that I observe them from.

The awful smell of Mole comes between us.

Was it Mendelssohn? he asks.

Yes, yes. There is more we could say, or I could. I am still finding my way on the clarinet and, while praise is hard to come by, I can't stay for another second. The shit smell is in my throat.

More generally, their smell is not like ours. It would be if they washed themselves properly, but they don't. And so it's a mulch of skin and dung, riper than sheep shit. It alarms everyone, reminding us all of what we need to be on our guard against—the threat of disease and hard times. Otherwise, look, this is what will happen. You will end up rolling around in your own waste.

In the hotel we have toilets. Porcelain with wood-crafted seats. We flush away our mess and it is forgotten. The strangers must live with theirs. It is a constant reminder of their difference, and at the same time it makes them more grimly familiar than we would like.

In the afternoon I tend the garden around the cage. I pull out the weeds, cut the grass around the stone rabbit. The whole time I am aware of the strangers' eyes boring into me. Silence is their only weapon—and I understand it—since they have something that we want.

It is quite amusing really. The way we have changed places. Now I am the one behind the wire. Someone of higher privilege on his hands and knees rearranging nature.

If I look up to return their interest, they look away. Or they close their eyes, squeeze them like a child does to make the ghosts disappear.

After an hour's weeding my knees are damp from the soft grass and the smell of onion weed is all over my hands.

I helped put the new lawn down last autumn when I first

9

arrived at the hotel. The grass still has a delicate spongy feel to it. Though inside the cage, where the strangers pace up and down, the grass is wearing thin. It is annoying, but there is nothing I can do about it.

Doctor has been waiting patiently for me to look up, to trap my attention.

We would very much like a bath, he says.

He makes it sound so entirely reasonable, as if we might just lift the roof off the cage and lower a bath in from a hotel window.

There is a tap near the cage, with a hose attached. We try to use what is close to hand. The Trustees are forever encouraging this kind of initiative.

I unwind the hose and push the nozzle into the feeding hole.

Immediately Mole begins hauling the hose in, hand over hand, until it lies in a coil on the floor of the cage.

It is a strange sight. The hose, I mean. I said so later to the Trustees. To see a bit of our world enter theirs.

I tell the strangers they have ten minutes.

This is how things happen. A new event is hatched and suddenly rules need to be invented.

Mole strips off his rags, his bits hang thinly off him. Naked, he is even more shaggy-haired. His pink toes are a marvel given how close he is to the shitting area.

A nod from Doctor and I turn on the tap for him to play the water over the other's bare skin. Mole winces and balls his fists, he shuts his eyes and holds up his hands in surrender as his cock shrivels. Now he must lift each foot in turn out of a growing puddle, then, without anywhere to place it he returns it to the mud.

I wonder, says Doctor, if we might have soap.

Soap is a reasonable request. But it means I have to drop everything and go inside, up the stairs to Supplies past the shared bathroom on the first-floor landing. The soaps for the hotel rooms are mean little slabs. I think it is fair to give the strangers one each, which is more than the other guests receive.

When I pass the cakes of soap through the feeding hole, Doctor is grateful.

You have a minute and twenty-five seconds left, then I'm turning off the water, I tell him.

Doctor doesn't bother with peeling off his rags—there's no time—but runs the hose over his head until it is a grey slick.

'Time!'

I turn off the tap. Doctor is dripping wet as he passes the nozzle of the hose through the feeding hole. I must pull it free and be quick about it, just in case he tries to bite me.

By the time I roll up the hose and loop it over the tap, Doctor is sitting on the ground looking composed and patient while Mole searches in his parted hair for lice.

I suppose it is obvious, but this is the point I wish to make to the Trustees. Since grooming is an immensely social activity I want to recommend that the cakes of soap listed under 'expenses' be considered 'social items' as much as 'hygiene items'.

Later, their teacups are ready to be collected. They have been left neatly on the floor of the cage beneath the feeding hole.

As I reach through, Mole drops his foot onto my wrist and pins it there. Doctor calls something, a rebuke—and as my wrist is released, Mole pushes his face to the bars.

He speaks in that quiet insistent way of his.

We wish to get on our way. We wish to go.

3

I won't say anything about this incident to the Trustees. I know what will result. Around the table a thought will light up at my failing to take proper precautions. I will be thought sloppy.

So, when they ask about changes in behaviour, without going into details, I let them know the strangers are still unpredictable.

Once a week the Trustees meet in the hotel 'library'. There are still a few shelves stocked with books, and although they are never read they contribute to an atmosphere that is thoughtful and considered. There is a log in the fire grate, but it is never lit. The chimney, now regarded a fire risk, even after years of safely blazing away, has been sealed.

The Trustees include my uncle and his wife, Dawn. It would be hard to exclude them given the hotel's association with the strangers. The other Trustees have been gathered from the ranks of the community-minded. The ever-dependent Mr Wooten, and the engineer from the hydro, Mr Bennett, who is also the chair. Mr Hughes from the grocery across the road. The retired angler, at whose request I record in the ledger as 'Mr Fish'. I know Mr Byrd the best. He has the secondhand bookshop in the old granary—three floors of creaking boards given over to crime fiction.

When I first came to live in the hotel Dawn took me along to Byrd's Books with the aim of burying my grief in someone else's. I had my first conversation with Mr Byrd in the bookshop, and right away I warmed to him. The twinkle in his eye sought to include me. He pressed his large hands down on the glass counter to ask if crime was my thing. I told him I'd never read a crime book before, an admission that sounded disappointing even to my own ears.

I like animals, I said.

He tapped the counter and looked away. I could see him thinking, did he have a book that featured a giraffe with a knife stuck in its throat?

The Trustees meet weekly.

As usual, they seek assurances. They pretend that where I bravely venture is a foreign land inaccessible to them. And so they ask questions, the answers to which they would know if they spent a little time in the backyard observing the strangers.

Are they sufficiently comfortable?

Yes, I reply. As far as I know, and under the circumstances, which, of course, are trying.

The strangers spend a great deal of their time sitting with their knees drawn up against their chests. Each looks after his own warmth in that regard. When there is little sunshine they will lie on the ground and curl up in a foetal position. Sometimes at night one will clutch the other in front, and once he is warm they will change positions. They have become so adept that, even while still asleep, they manage to roll over without waking or causing a disturbance.

13

You see all this? asks Dawn.

When I can't sleep. Yes.

Or else they lie on their sides, reaching in their sleep for what is not there. In the cold light of dawn they will stretch out a hand to pull something back over themselves. Old instincts, I imagine. The older one wriggles his hips, working himself deeper into the dirt.

Has there been anything untoward about their behaviour? asks Mr Hughes. He rolls a pen nervously between his fingers. I wish he wouldn't smirk. It makes me feel like I am lying when I am not.

Untoward? Well, there is the matter of their toilet.

Yes, yes, he says quickly. No, I was thinking of something else. Did anyone read about that pelican that repeatedly bashed its head against its cage until it brought about its death?

It suicided? Really, Frank? Where on earth did such a thing happen?

I can't recall. Canada? Or was it here? Do we have pelicans?

The Trustees look around the room for the answer.

We have them at the zoo, I point out.

I have something more to say about this.

Can we claim as our own any of the creatures at the zoo? I say. They have been chosen precisely because of their exoticism. Otherwise there would be little point in putting into cages what is already at liberty in the neighbourhood.

Silence. Apart from a wrapper coming off a barley sugar. I put a bowl out ahead of each meeting.

Still, says Mr Byrd. To bash yourself to death would require superhuman quantities of determination.

It was a pelican, though, says Mr Hughes. I thought I said.

14

Yes, but, I'm just drawing attention to a level of determination needed to overcome every instinct rallying in the other direction. Life, and life at any cost.

At this point I feel I must speak up again.

There has been no talk of suicide, if that is what you're getting at, I say.

Of course not, says Uncle Warwick. Why would they?

Did the pelican have a name, Frank?

It was a pelican, that's all I know.

Mr Bennett looks around the table.

Any other business? he asks.

A drumroll of fingers on the table from Mr Fish, he looks up the table at Mr Bennett.

Yesterday, he says. Yesterday I came across a lovely length of birch on the riverbank. I immediately thought of the strangers. It was too big for me to handle on my own. Fortunately, a couple of other anglers were fishing nearby. They gave a hand and I was able to bring it back with me.

Together we carry and drag the branch around the side of the hotel to the backyard. It is surprisingly heavy, but the angler was right. It looks ideal. But with a little work to it first. And Mr Hughes has to run across the road for his saw.

After a trim, the branch is ready to fit through the feeding hole. I am more used to shoving a teaspoon of egg through that space. Now we push in the thick end. The hole is big enough.

The strangers pull and wrestle it the rest of the way through, then they let go and step clear for the log to bounce onto the ground of the cage. It is oddly satisfying, especially to those who said it could be done, and amazing to those who said it couldn't.

Doctor raises his foot and nudges the birch until it finds its rightful resting place. Then, to everyone's delight, with a bit of theatrical *la dee dah*, he sits down on it—wary at first, hands out to his sides, before his face settles to a smile. Mole, however, is still on his feet, his mouth set against itself. His resentment threatening to sour the occasion until Doctor pats the place on the birch beside himself.

He seems to understand the younger one's steam. Sees it all somehow.

'Here.'

That's all he says, and Mole turns as meek as a lamb to go and sit down beside him, and we all cheer.

It is not easy to think up useful things that can be done for them, and so, when something like the log comes along, it turns into something we can all draw satisfaction from.

There are other small joys. A quicksilver movement along the top of the garden wall and Doctor's eyes bob with each delicate hop taken by the finch. The bristled eyebrow, the crosshatch of thought in that rudely night-plastered face of his. He is moved. He is. The bird bobbing in his eye, it too just seemed to drop out of the sky.

This morning, after I passed a cup of black tea through to Doctor, he held onto the cup but did not take it from me. He held it the way we hold our hands over a fire.

Please, he asked. Is there any news? A woman in a hat I believe…from the agency?

No. I am afraid there is nothing new to report.

We had hoped to hear from her by now.

Yes. I am aware.

Well, is there any news about our release?

That, again.

His eyes trace an old life in the sky.

What do we know? We know that something happened. Something so terrible that they are unable, or unwilling, to describe it to us. Something big and terrible. At various times of the night we wake with the idea that the catastrophe the strangers fled is now rolling towards us.

What is known so far is based on overheard snippets. Some of it volunteered. There is a before and after. There was a catastrophe that no one else survived. As to what happened next, they have been more forthcoming.

What to do?

They must walk. As survivors they walk in a stunned state, and place all trust in the road to deliver them to safety.

At the rising sound of traffic they step onto the shoulder of the road and wait for it to rush by, a line of faces in the side-windows, a stream of unconcern, then the countryside drops back into place. Some whispering from the end of season corn-stalks, blackened, and fibrous. Scampering mice. Fossicking birds. The stickiness of the road at noon. A rag flaps on a scarecrow, the breeze dies, and the scarecrow slumps in the broken corn. All that we are familiar with.

The strangers move on. The younger one with a long hopeful stride. The older one slowed by thoughtful distraction as much as by his stolen moccasin and laceless boot.

Now and then they stop to look back. There is the bend in the road that they came around. Beyond it, a greying memory of more road.

There are plenty of encouraging signs for the traumatised

strangers to note. The relentless pasture. The thrust of gorse grown rampant. The bustling certainty of the clouds. It is the world getting on with itself.

Two nights are passed in a railway carriage hauled to a farm paddock and left there. They wake to drifts of cobwebs and pale light. The upholstery and windows provide a measure of comfort, but no destination, and late one afternoon they head back out to the road.

On they go, in the belief that a new life will eventually grow around them.

They live as wild animals do. They kneel on all fours to drink from creeks, they steal from orchards. They make their beds in culverts, in ditches, on cold beds of gravel. They wriggle under bushes, clasping their knees to their chests to hold a ball of heat to themselves.

One dusk they follow three deer and a fawn along a dry creek bed in the direction of lights sprinkled on a dark hillside. In the morning they climb out of the undergrowth up onto the road.

Almost immediately a driver stops to offer them a lift.

But the same unanswerable question arrives—a lift to where? They do not know this country. They have no idea what lies ahead, around the next bend, beyond that hill, across that river. How can they sensibly nominate a destination?

The puzzled driver closes his window, and the car accelerates away until the scrape of their footwear on the road is the only sound they hear.

More houses now. Lawns. A dog runs out the end of a driveway to lick and slobber over their boots.

A woman with clippers stares over a hedge. She doesn't

know what to make of them. A long time ago, as a child, she remembers men in a state of worldly abandonment turning up at the farmhouse for a bed and a meal in exchange for bringing in the corn or docking lambs, mending fences if they knew how. But these strangers don't have the same fevered eyes. They look back, interested for a second, at the woman with the clippers, and then the moment passes, the opportunity to say something, to offer directions or even a cup of tea.

In a dozen different ways the strangers are spun onto our world—until one morning they wake to discover the patch of grass they passed the night on is a traffic island.

A trumpet blares, then a bandleader in a white tunic marches around the corner twirling a baton that glitters and glows. Near the traffic island with its two castaways, she comes to a halt, and, lifting her knees with perfect timing, she marches on the spot. On both sides of the street, the crowd cheers with approval and she marches on with her smile lighting up the day, the trumpet blaring at her rear.

It is the town's anniversary.

Here at last the strangers might have recognised where they had arrived. The retail faces of the crowd. Pedestrian crossings. Traffic lights. Shopfronts. Powerlines. All those things that announce civilisation. But any relief they might have felt quickly wanes under the pressures of stomachs grinding with hunger and nature's more urgent calls.

At the first opportunity they cross the road and hurry down a side lane which brings them to another part of the procession. A float, a construction of hair piled three metres high, the tresses parted to pink varnished skin and a sea of blazing doll eyes. These are eyes that cannot see, that do not care. Small children point and jump up and down delighted to have a part of their own world honoured with a place in the procession.

Men in tractors rumble by. A truck tows a float piled with hay bales and a girl bottle-feeding a lamb.

Another street delivers the strangers to the end of the procession, and here they tag onto a long and weary line of people in unseasonable coats, carrying infants and battered suitcases. Their faces are drained, they do not speak, and some in the crowd wonder if these people began their journey in the wintry north, lured by the promise of new beginnings among our sunburnt hills.

The strangers might have recognised themselves in the clothes worn by those in the procession. Grimy clothes that looked to have been pulled from any old place. They are happier in this company. They feel less conspicuous.

Their problem is where to look. What or whom may they look at? Slowly they catch up with the fact that they have forfeited that right. They are part of the procession. Their role is to be looked at. This is what happens. They have broken their moorings. They have drifted. Now there is a price to pay for not being local. Now they must be prepared to be stared at.

For hours they follow the sloped shoulders of those in front, as the procession winds in and out of unfamiliar streets beneath the grim conduct of buildings closed for the weekend.

Near the square they break away to sip at the fountain. A line of sparrows edges sideways to make room. In bright sunshine the heavy-coated strangers duck their heads, splash water over their faces, rub the grime off their necks, and, after filling water bottles, hurry back to their place in the procession.

Late in the afternoon those leading the procession cross

the finish line. They wander back against the flow carrying sponsors' T-shirts and sandwiches, and at this point, the procession begins to lose its shape and the strangers return to the familiar question: where to now?

They decide to throw their luck in with several others carrying suitcases, but soon it is clear that these people are as lost as they are.

They may have noticed too that they are viewed differently. They are still looked at, but with less delight. Were they not just part of the procession? Why are they not still part of it?

Or, to ask the same thing in a slightly more blunt way—what are they doing here?

People now stop to stare at the two strangers. Mothers turn the heads of their children away. Cars slow down.

The older one appears to walk with a limp. Mr Hughes will later speak of one foot lifting, as though balancing a feather on its toe. The other foot is slammed down.

The lights turn green, but the traffic stays put.

On the east side, among the old warehouses in the black hole of town, the strangers encounter others who, on the face of it, appear to be like themselves—living rough in the cracks and shadows.

Who could blame anyone for thinking the strangers were more of the same. Look at their clothes. And, in turn, the strangers may have wondered if this is only what people saw—thieves unable to conceal their theft.

With darkness falling they stop finally outside a hotel with its flickering sign, 'All Welcome'.

And this is how, three months ago, they came to enter our world.

4

It was obvious they had come from a place far away. Two scarecrows. That's what they looked like. As if they had come through a firestorm of other peoples' lives. Bits of those lives had stuck to them, a footprint, a glance, a hope. They were in themselves not anyone in particular. Nothing in their clothing matched. They were unshaven. A grey stubble covered a rash on the older one's face. His trousers were too big. He wore a moccasin and a boot with an unlaced tongue that flapped. The younger stranger's boots were in better condition—but filthy, and only one boot had laces. His arms climbed out of the sleeves of a jacket several sizes too small for him. His shirt, to judge by the inside collar, had once been white. His black trousers ended at his shins.

Momentarily the monotony of the hotel was enlivened by the spectacle of their arrival.

We watched them climb the stairs to their rooms. The older one was slow. His movement heavy, as if he were wading upriver. His moccasin kept catching on a strip of metal set into the edge of each carpeted stair, until he took hold of the banister, removed the moccasin and lifted his foot clear.

That's when we all saw it. His naked foot, under the

chandelier and against the gleam of the polished wood. The disgusting moccasin in his hand. What a lonesome sight they were. Startled by everything, even by the serene eyes and antlers of the deer mounted on the wall at the top of the stairs. The deer had never looked as outlandish as it did at the moment the strangers stopped to gaze up at it. Not once had we ever considered where the rest of the deer was, or stopped to think about it at another stage of life, as a fawn, say, when it is impossible for such a creature to know its future.

The strangers moved slowly in the closed air, across the soft carpet, their eyes shifting at the muffled and sometimes exuberant sound of lavatories flushing behind the panelled walls, of water rudely running through pipes.

In the upstairs hall I caught up with their smell, a weave of old leaves, dirt and sweat.

I pointed out the shared bathroom, the toilet, the showers.

The word 'showers' caused the older stranger to blink. Pale blue eyes beneath a tangle of grey eyebrow.

At the door to their room I held up the key. I was expecting one or the other to take it. But something unexpected happened. A point Dawn would later dwell on.

You say they stepped away?

Yes. The older one, primly, with his hands held behind his back, as if he were a ordinary paying guest. He waited while I inserted the key.

You saw all that?

Yes.

Then what?' she asked.

Well, they entered the room, but again, with the same anticipation as any paying guest.

They looked around, then went to the window. The younger one placed himself to one side, and drew back the curtain.

I switched on the overhead light, and the strangers threw their hands up. I quickly apologised. Electric light. They weren't used to it.

Next they discovered the closet. They both stared politely at the hangers.

Your beds, I said.

They looked at them without much interest. The younger one took the bed by the door. The older stranger sat down on the one near the window. They were like workmen who at the end of a long day fall silent.

Picture a scene with a life raft—it is still sinking as its two survivors stagger up a shingle beach. Safely ashore, the survivors look back out to sea, but they cannot find a trace of their boat. Under the circumstances they might struggle to explain how they made it to shore. The facts may seem quite unreasonable. The survivors continue to speak of a life raft, but where is it?

At the reception desk, Uncle Warwick asked the strangers where they had come from—their addresses were needed for the register. The older one cradled the desk pen in his fingers. He looked thoughtful. Then he shook his head, at a loss, he explained, as to what to put down.

Your address, Uncle Warwick said again.

Yes. Yes. I understand the question. But I don't have the answer, neither of us does. We no longer have an address.

They had no credit cards, no documents, no proof of identity. In the end they didn't sign the register, since what was the point of signing under a name and providing an address that belonged to a place that no longer existed?

Uncle Warwick was still bewildered as he stood in the foyer under the chandelier recounting his conversation with the strangers.

They had no money either.

Something about their situation had made him place their needs ahead of his own. And now I had a view of my uncle at the moment when he and Dawn had understood that they would have to take me in as I had nowhere else to go.

Six months earlier I had shuffled through the same door as the strangers.

My change of circumstances had come about so unexpectedly that I was still in a numb state as Dawn led me down to the ground floor. Or the 'garden room', as she called it.

A door opened onto a desk and chair. An unfriendly looking bed was shoved up against the wall at one end. The musty air shifted as Dawn pulled back the curtains. The long grass looked in.

I was aware some gratitude was expected, but I could not manage it, not at that moment.

I could only think to ask who else had lived down here in the basement.

You're the first, she said.

Yet there was the made bed, and a pair of curtains that stopped at the windowsill, like eyelids.

Dawn told me that a room responds to the personality of its occupant. She'd seen it happen often enough in the hotel. She believed it would be no different down here. The room and I would grow together. Very soon, she promised, it would feel like home.

Dawn smiled, gauging the effect of her words. I didn't want to put her to any trouble.

I'll be all right. Thank you, Dawn, I said.

Oh, I am sure you will be, she said. Everything will come right. You'll see.

Her smile was determined to block out all the misfortune the world had to offer.

I felt dead, and that was all there was to it. The dead should not be poked and prodded for signs of life. I listened to her feet climbing the stairs. I have an idea my uncle was waiting at the top. I heard a male voice mumble and then the door to the lobby closed.

I sat down on the edge of the bed. This was not my room. The life was flattened out of the pillows. When I lay down I could not find a familiar groove. I might as well have lain on top of another's body. When I woke the next morning, I could feel the weight of the hotel bearing down on me. I had the strangest feeling of coming to after a particularly vivid dream to find myself not yet arrived in wakefulness.

There was the hard lacquer of newness and unfamiliarity, and every movement, getting out of bed and even getting myself up the stairs, required me to push against it.

I was reminded of this struggle the first morning the strangers came down to the dining room. In a hotel, each moment is a borrowed one, from the chair sat in to the air breathed. I saw that in the strangers, the way they tentatively raised the cutlery. They were wary of the air, of disturbing it or the other guests in the dining room. They didn't wish to take more than what they felt they were entitled to.

No one in the dining room dared to speak. Ears strained to hear what the strangers at the corner table said.

Within a few days the 'celebrities'—for that is what the strangers had turned into—didn't so much move around us as we did around them, as filings around a magnet. Children ran up to touch them, then ran off with the delight of having stolen something they could not make proper sense of.

Wherever the strangers turned they were met with bashful smiles. On the heels of living in the wild it must have been exhausting for them.

The older one was better at it. The right thing to say flowed effortlessly from him at exactly the right moment. The younger one's face wouldn't settle. The idea of all this attention, I thought, and that it was happening to him of all people.

Of course, everyone hoped to hear something that would explain the preposterous sight of the two tramps passing the salt and pepper to one another with a grace that surprised those of us peeking in from the side door. I wondered if their manners were a matter of survival, old habits, since that is what had got me through my early days in the hotel with Uncle Warwick and Dawn.

I shared with the strangers an easy lapse into daydreaminess, a sign taken by Dawn that I was unhappy. I was not completely so.

The hotel world was busier and more social than the one I had left behind. But when I considered what I had left behind, Mum and Dad, and the world we had shared, that space was enormous, and by its absence it continued to make itself felt.

In a hotel there are endless details to attend to. If Uncle

Warwick was held up on the phone he would wave to his new pair of hands to take over—a toenail had been found in a bed, an unflushed toilet was causing concern. A hotel room must greet a guest as if he or she is the first ever to have slept in it. A pubic hair on a bathroom tile will shatter the illusion. Suddenly the bathroom has a history, and the wounded face at the door is, like every other, making a case for its own distress.

We worried that the strangers might leave too much of their history in their room. Uncle Warwick worried that he would have to burn their sheets once they got on their way.

We weren't sure when that might be.

That first evening everyone in the dining room ordered cauliflower and cheese sauce. It caused panic in the kitchen. Of course there weren't enough cauliflowers until Mr Hughes arrived in the lobby clutching a sackful.

But what else was there to share with the strangers? The locals ate with the faith of the blind dipping their bodies into baptismal water—or in this case, cauliflower cheese sauce. The room trembled on the clipped movement of knives and forks. When the strangers leaned towards one another to share a confidence the entire room leaned with them. Faces looked up. Nobody wanted to miss anything.

As the strangers stood to leave, there was the scraping of chair legs across the dining room.

Near the door the older one stopped to look back. His instinct was right. His face reported the terrible news. He looked oppressed. Which meant, of course, we had become his oppressors. Anyone in the dining room that night would have been astonished to hear themselves described in this way.

As the diners filed out, some at least had enough dignity to look foolish. There was a lot of grinning, but they couldn't stop from gathering on the hotel verandah, where, at one end, the strangers had invitingly parked themselves.

Everyone took an interest in the night sky. No one could find much to say. The night was a dull grey, with darker flat linings, a thin moon, a few stars to hold the eye. And, insufficient light to see the strangers slip away—until a voice cried out 'There!'

Whose? It doesn't matter. Some collective fear of ours had suddenly found its voice.

Now, everyone peered after the shadows disappearing up the drive. Were the strangers getting away?

We heard that peculiar scrape and slide of their footwear, a bit rushed, a bit more urgent.

Someone burst after them. Then everyone was on the charge—Dawn with her tray of tea was brushed aside—as word got around that they were getting away.

But from who or what? Nobody thought to ask.

The strangers began to run.

The curious thing is that we knew what to do. As did the strangers, whose stride lengthened out on the street. The younger one took hold of the older one's arm to hurry him along.

Those of us chasing didn't share a word. But what could any of us have said to encourage the idea that we had a plan? How might we have explained our actions to ourselves?

A mob of sheep, frozen to the spot, will wait for one or the other to decide what to do. Is it safe? Is there danger? Then one decides, and all, in effect, have decided. The mob rushes off, those at the rear scrambling madly after, terrified to be left alone. Until, for whatever reason, the leaders stop, causing those behind to pull up. In a stunning reversal of authority they turn around to lead the former leaders back to where they came from, nodding their way through the gates as if their foray into a neighbouring paddock was now cause for regret, a supreme act of folly.

The strangers reached an intersection and there they lost us. Maybe they meant to divide us, because that is what happened. We swarmed around a corner and stopped. Then everyone took it in turn to look up, puzzled by their involvement. We peered into the dark. The last of the diners were still arriving by the time those in front had turned back.

A moment later everyone was splitting off down side streets and lanes to their beds.

I wandered back to the hotel with Mr Byrd and Mr Hughes, discussing the strange event we had been part of. No one had anything sensible to say.

In the morning, the strangers were down at breakfast, unfolding their table napkins over their laps.

5

On the sixth day after the strangers arrived, I was clearing away their breakfast dishes when the older one asked if I knew the way to the mayor's office. He explained that they wished to ask for residency.

We were flattered—it was the celebrated air, of course. We knew it to be world-class. Thanks to the strangers we now breathed more deeply.

The mayor's office is off the square, near where the strangers had lost us. It is a ten-minute brisk walk. I offered to take them there.

On our way through town I seemed to slip from view. All eyes were on the strangers. People felt some sort of provisional connection, as if they had slowed down to gape at a car accident. Greedy eyes fell upon the older one's moccasin, and in the next moment they climbed all over both strangers.

At the mayor's office the old problem was revisited. They had no documentation. Residency could not be extended to ghosts. And, so, no forms were filled out.

I showed the disappointed strangers out of the building. The morning sun struck their stunned faces. They looked up and down the street. It was clear they had run out of road.

On our way back to the hotel we stopped for the younger one to tie up his one boot that had laces. While he was crouching down, the older stranger found his reflection in a shop window. He steadied himself, then reached up to where a button was missing on his shirt. His hand dropped to a length of string acting as a trouser belt. He gave it a tug, and grunted.

Were their clothes stolen? I asked, making a joke. Were they pinched off a clothesline?

The older one was not at all offended. Their clothes, he replied, belonged to others who in a moment of great misfortune had lost everything, all their possessions, in some cases even their skins.

Years ago, when I was twelve, our class visited a lighthouse. It stood on the point, like something out of a storybook. Cylindrical walls, glossy white paint. It had a surprising feeling of lightness and elevation combined with a resilience to withstand whatever catastrophic weather event was thrown against it. One hundred and forty-seven stone steps climbed to a glassed-in room, a tiny space commanding the ocean.

Even then, as young as I was, certain things had come to mind: light, aloneness, a desire to glimpse what could not be seen.

Everyone had a different idea about what the strangers' catastrophe might be. Some even saw it as a coming event, and looked forward to it in a perverse kind of way. The same mad desire that leads some of us, apparently, to drive to the coast the moment a tsunami warning is broadcast.

Bill Francis, who owns all the land from the river as far as the hills in the east—sheep and cattle mainly—took the strangers up in his plane to look for the catastrophe. Uncle Warwick asked me to go in his place. Bill laughed when I told him my uncle was too busy. I found out later he hates flying.

Bill warned us that there might be a few bumps on the way up. His weather-beaten face cracked open into a confident smile as we lifted and bumped against something that we could not see. It was air. But it seemed to deserve another name.

The plane lurched and we rose in our seats and dropped down again. It was frightening, but also bewildering, because what was there to attach our fear to? Just air, apparently.

The strangers sat in front of me, shoulder to shoulder, unperturbed.

We all wore headphones. You flicked a switch to hear and another to speak. Bits of sun-dashed farmland slid out from under cloud. Ahead of us rose cruel ridges with a history of turning men's hipbones to powder and of breaking working dogs. Their jagged peaks promised to meet our expectations, but as we flew over them they flattened out to rock, windswept grass and slopes riddled with sheep tracks, and slips caused by erosion. Hills shaped like knuckles bruised the sky. Hills as bare as ironing boards, their crowns over-proud of their faint achievement. Grass. Topsoil. Scatterings of lime rock.

We flew over hobby farms. Tar drives and swimming pools set in paddocks that for a century or longer sheep and cattle had grazed over. That first summer of drought after the life-stylers moved in, thirsty cattle had walked through fences in search of fresh grass and water. After a call from an irate neighbour Dad sent me off to retrieve a steer found standing at a swimming pool, gazing at its own likeness.

The wing on my side lifted, and far below a burst of sunlight hit a stretch of road, no bigger than a toothpick. Bill straightened up the plane and for a time we followed two long green trucks on their way to the slaughterhouse.

I had travelled that road as a child, hour after hour, as my father gripped the steering wheel with fearsome single-mindedness. Until finally we arrived at a farm gate that I had to get out to open.

This was a strange new chore, one I fumbled at. My father smiled a kindly warning that I could expect an endless amount of fumbling in this new world we had arrived in. He drove through, his arm hanging out the window. I was to shut the gate. It was very important that I not forget. We bumped along a broken stretch of narrow road. Slabs of tarseal, dirt, shingle. Every new bend pushing us onto a new patch of hillside with white dots all over it. Even the sheep seemed part of the plot. I thought my father had made a terrible mistake, that a crazy light in his eye had led us astray. And now, look—there was a wire fence around us, and I could not decide if we were inside it or outside.

A huge bank of cloud up ahead indicated the dividing ranges. We climbed—crawled as if up a pane of glass, then slid off the edge of the cloud. As we turned for home, the younger stranger looked back. He ripped off his headphones. The older stranger did the same and leaned across for the younger one to shout something in his ear. He yelled behind his hand. Whatever the stranger said caused the older one to turn in the direction of the cloud.

34

I thought there might be something there. I waited until the strangers were facing the front before I looked. But what I saw was only cloud. I searched for a figure in a chariot carrying a trident, but the bank of cloud could not even manage that. No one could say what the catastrophe looked like.

On our descent, the picture below began to crumble and wash away to bits and pieces.

We bounced lightly onto the airstrip at Bill Francis's farm, a steady drone still in our ears. As I stepped from the plane all I could hear was the clicking of a single cicada.

Near the landing strip, a number of farmhands standing in a line outside a kill shed threw down their smokes. Whatever they had been discussing was casually let go as they stiffened up to receive the VIPs. They were more used to examining the land. At such moments they might even have considered themselves to be lords of it. But, in the company of the farmer, they found themselves returned to the land differently. They became part of its brokenness, and its imperfections found a match in their own fraying collars, scratched skin, abrasions, and careless efforts at shaving.

As the younger stranger crossed my line of sight he merged with the farmhands and but for the fact he was already known to me I would not have been able to tell him apart.

I noticed he did not balk at the sight of a severed sheep's head lying in the grass. I looked to see if the older stranger had noticed.

Up in Bill Francis's plane it was as if the entire world was knowable, as it stretched from edge to edge, with tidy coloured-in rectangles and squares of green with yellow fringes. Up there we could see everything and remain untouched by it. It was like being at the movies.

We had flown over the old farmhouse. Tiny from the air, and inconsequential, the paddocks too small and fanciful for the glories my father had dreamt up for them.

Then I saw the car—just the roof, sitting in the bush, like a bottle top and far below a corner it had safely driven round on a hundred other occasions. And I remembered my father's red face at my bedroom door.

Why don't you jump in the car, he said.

No.

You're not coming then?

Still not coming, I said.

I didn't want to waste the afternoon at the hotel. Nothing anyone did or said there was private. My uncle would be out to perform as usual. I would have to adjust to a louder version of him as he put Dad down. He liked to present his mad farmer brother, who he claimed didn't know a cow's tit from a tom tit, to the drinkers in the bar. His brother who couldn't, he said, even catch all his own whiskers with a razor let alone shear a sheep. My father would just grin, the way he did when driving a long stretch. He said he'd only worry if he thought anything Warwick said was true.

But I didn't need to hear all that again, or to add myself to my uncle's audience.

I said to Dad, No, you go. You and Mum. Say hello to Uncle Warwick and Dawn for me.

I went on attaching the reed to my clarinet. I didn't look up. I knew what his expression would be.

36

Years ago, a second-hand, pale-blue bike was wheeled up the hallway for my ninth birthday. Its soldered joints bubbled beneath the thick enamel paint. I loved it instantly. But my father was in a rage because it had been delivered to the house with flat tyres. He had rung the shop to complain.

His rage had poured out of him in a confused, molten state—love, anger, responsibility, indignation, each thing clinging to the other. But rage was all that could be heard.

He drove off with Mum in that same swollen state.

Early evening I sat in the kitchen waiting for them to return and watched the shadows creep across the floor. A stillness whispered to me. Pay attention. Pay attention to the corner of the window above the sink. Pay attention to the spider and the shift of cloud and the illumination of the cobweb in the light.

The knock on the door was Uncle Warwick looking grave. He dropped a hand onto my shoulder, clutched it, and told me to pack some clothes.

I thought it would be just for the night. But then he said, 'And your clarinet.'

We drove to the hotel in silence, headlights burning into the dusk. Soon the lights of town reached out to us, one by one, then in a cluster, and suddenly we were in tight streets lined with houses whose windows blazed.

Uncle Warwick drove more slowly than usual, slowed by thought. His eyes were soft. As if he weren't really looking at the road.

I was an unexpected problem. His brother's son. His nephew. Bound to me by the complexity of family, in a role he had never taken seriously. In fact, it made him more reserved, more circumspect, as if family was a mirror designed to reduce his big easy-going hotel character.

On the edge of town we stopped at the lights, and he turned to ask if I thought I could handle fish and chips. No. I didn't think I could. I wasn't hungry—I couldn't imagine feeling hungry ever again—but I thanked him. I could not remember another occasion when my uncle had sought my opinion. I hear you, Sport, he said. He wasn't hungry either. The lights turned green, and we drove on, as silent as before, but with a bit more speed on the gear shifts as we neared the hotel.

6

The clarinet was part of an estate never claimed by the family of a hotel guest who lay dead a day and a half in an upstairs bed. My uncle gave it to me one Christmas.

It came in a long flat case, in parts, each in its own snug velvet bed. I connected them but I couldn't make a sound. Then it clicked. The reed needs to sit against the mouthpiece. It is like fitting a tongue to the roof of a mouth. The lip of the mouthpiece sits just a whisker longer than the reed.

The learning process is long, and cannot be hurried. And, as I have found with the clarinet, competence is built on many tiny steps, its inner music waits to be discovered.

I learned to play a flute at school, from a teacher who had shown us how to blow through a blade of grass to make it whistle. The flute felt like a natural progression of the grasslands that whispered in our ears day and night at the farm.

In itself the wind is hard to hear. It has to occupy other things. It needs a split gable to rush through. Clapboard or loose windows to play and slap against. Clouds to push about. Without these, the wind is just a bully that we have heard of.

This is the space the catastrophe also occupies. To pinpoint it any further we would have liked to see the smoke and flames.

I carried the breakfast tray up to the strangers' room in my socks. I put the tray down. Put my ear to the door. I hoped to hear something—like horse hooves or a cannon.

But all I heard was the deep silence of sleep.

There was no bridge across, no language to bring the strangers' experience into our lives.

We continued to wait patiently.

And, in the course of a week, the strangers slipped into a state of important aloneness. Shipwrecked figures asked to make sense of—not the place they had arrived at, but the one left behind. And we were shaped by an event that we could not see or talk about—both the strangers and ourselves.

I realise I am attempting to build a world out of language, the very same thing that the strangers say is too blunt an instrument to describe what happened to them.

But what else is there? At least my ledger entries hold out a promise of some future understanding, which is also the hope of the Trust—that, eventually, a picture of the catastrophe will emerge.

One morning, after clearing the breakfast tables, I came in on a conversation between the strangers and my uncle. Uncle Warwick stopped to acknowledge me. The strangers, however, barely registered me.

You were saying? said the older one.

Yes, continued my uncle, the guest in question had seen a remarkable thing himself. At an hour when the rest of us were asleep he stood in the backyard under the night sky and when he looked up he saw the blazing tail of a comet.

The older stranger smiled. And when the guest said he'd seen a comet, what did you think he had seen?

Why, a comet, replied Warwick.

Precisely. A word is supplied and as a result you saw. But we have no such word at our disposal.

We wondered if the strangers might make something with their hands. There was some discussion of materials. Thread was favoured early on. It is light and flexible. It doesn't declare any part of itself to be greater than another part. It has infinity on its side. Fishing line had some support. Then someone suggested fencing wire and that felt right, more us.

Bill Francis sent his lead hand, Joe Phillips, to the hotel with a coil of fencing wire and a pair of pliers. I lugged the materials up to the strangers' room. The younger one took the coil of wire, nodded 'thanks' and closed the door.

Two afternoons went by, then everyone was summoned to the dining room. Viktor, the kitchenhand, me from the basement. Uncle Warwick and Dawn were already there. The strangers too, of course. Even the brat, Warwick and Dawn's girl, Katie.

A white bed sheet covered an object the size of an apple box.

At the older stranger's signal, Uncle Warwick nodded, and I lifted the sheet.

We stared—at first with hope, then with varieties of confusion. We went on staring. Smiling and staring. No one wanted to risk looking like a fool in front of everyone else.

It was a ball of wire. Not quite a ball. On the second or third inspection, I realised it would be quite wrong to call it that. Nor was it a square or a rectangle or any shape that you could put a name to. Yet it was something. It had shape, character, but not one we could describe. It was full of holes. Uniform ones, I would have said. But then I noticed a number that were irregular.

Of course the fault lay with us, because what we instinctively searched for was pattern, and there wasn't any.

Still, something needed to be said. The strangers waited.

Uncle Warwick stroked his lips. Dawn's tight smile stretched across her teeth. Her mouth parted as if ready to say something.

Then Viktor said he thought it looked like a tea strainer. No one said he was wrong.

At last, the older stranger put us out of our misery. The 'wire thing', he said, represents the conundrum they find themselves in—asked to describe a catastrophe which they cannot, asked to provide documentation which they lack, asked to speak of a place that no longer exists.

Right, said Uncle Warwick, and cast his eyes around to look for a place to display it. Suddenly everyone had an opinion. It ended up in the dining room, on the piano that no one ever plays.

A cat used to prowl the garden wall in the backyard. My uncle hates cats, and he is right—cats are killers.

In the first weeks of making my life in the room downstairs I'd look up from my clarinet and wonder what the clattering noise was—it turned out to be Uncle Warwick firing stones at the cat from the back door.

The cat would just stop and stare. Warwick was a hopeless shot. The cat drove him nuts. Then it disappeared.

Now the 'wire thing' sat there like a taunt, and agitated him like the cat had.

My uncle could not cross the dining room without stopping

to glare at it. But for it being indoors I'm sure he would have thrown a rock at it. He didn't like to think he was being made a fool of.

It was a talking point among other guests. Most ended up frowning at this problem that no one could solve.

We felt inadequate. We simply weren't up to it. And that inadequacy now sat at the centre of the hotel's life.

One evening Uncle Warwick invited the guests to offer a description of the conundrum.

A woman sitting with her elderly father rose. She managed, 'It looks like—' but was cut off by the older stranger.

He apologised, in his own way, but then explained that if we must say that something looks *like* something else then we miss the opportunity to say what it is.

But please continue, he said.

The woman shook her head and sat down. We were all numb, as if we were back in a classroom.

Well, I have a word, said someone at the rear. Mr Bennett, the engineer, got to his feet. He ignored the sea of eyes worried on his behalf. He concentrated on the shabby older stranger.

Death, he said.

The stranger nodded.

Colossal death, he said.

The air went out of the room. The walls curved round. Then a spoon clattered on the wooden floor, and a tremendous tension was released in the room.

People stood, grabbed their coats. They rudely pushed others out of the way. They surged out onto the street as if that was where safety lay.

How odd the evening had been. A stop-start affair filled

with small urgencies and fleeting sensations and another occasion now for our disappointment, as we stood in the foyer to watch the strangers troop upstairs to their room.

Who could blame them for staying there for longer spells? A whole afternoon or evening might pass without a sighting. We looked up the stairs—we waited—then went on with our tasks.

We wanted the strangers to be comfortable. We wanted them to be, well, more like us, if they could, and more responsive to our own willing faces. We wanted them to be available.

Instead, they moved around the hotel like ghosts. In their odd clothes they spooked guests enjoying a quiet moment in the library. They silenced drinkers in the bar, peering in from the door. They themselves did not drink. Their sobriety made my uncle uneasy. Dawn thought he took it much too personally. Alcohol loosens everyone's tongues, Uncle Warwick's in particular. The first time he offered the strangers whisky I saw that he had in mind a long evening when at last every door and window would fly open and it would be possible to see the catastrophe they had fled.

The strangers slipped from view. They stopped coming down to the dining room except in the evening and even then that couldn't always be counted on. This felt like an additional affront to my uncle who, so far, had been patient and generous. He stopped looking up the stairs for them, stopped being the happy innkeeper. Treated them as they apparently wished to be seen—as ghosts.

All that expectant air, useful at the start of a grand adventure, had gone.

That was when Uncle Warwick and Bill Francis began their phone calls, long conversations that drifted into the evening. My uncle, hunched at his desk in the little alcove, rubbing at his eyes, nodding.

7

The strangers had been at the hotel for fifteen days. The sixteenth night passed, and I woke to a tremendous racket of banging hammers. It seemed as if the world was about to cave in. Windows along the upper floor were slammed down. But there was no hiding from it. *Bang. Bang. Bang. Bang.* I pulled back my curtain and the fierce morning glare rushed inside.

Uncle Warwick and Bill Francis were out in the backyard. Bill's general tidiness added to the idea of his quiet competence, especially next to my uncle, red-face, sweat cupped under the arms of the shirt he usually wore inside the hotel, his belt loosened off to allow for the pour of his stomach.

The younger stranger was also out there, on top of the frame, perched like a cat, his long spine lined up with the roof beam as his thin arms pulled mesh over it.

The 'wire thing' which I was used to seeing on the piano, now sat on a dining-room chair on the lawn.

Uncle Warwick's explanation sounded entirely reasonable.

By scaling up 'the thing' he believed it might grow into a space for one and all to step inside where they could grasp for themselves *that* which mere words could not describe.

What appeared to be a right angle turned out not to be.

Curves flattened out betraying first impressions. But then when I looked again I rediscovered the curve. I found it easier to concentrate on the more familiar things—the sawhorse, the concrete mixer, the grey concrete hardening around the foundation posts, the rolls of mesh and fencing wire. All of it with names, all identifiable.

The structure did not have regular sides. Of course, that was the point. Everything about it defied regularity. There were openings that promised to lead somewhere, but it turned out to be a basket of air. Such as we had flown through in Bill Francis's plane, when we looked down at a view held together by air, and our eye, and a determination to join things up in our own particular way.

A small number of guests, men, came down to the backyard for a closer look. One or two declared it an aviary and set about convincing others of their view.

More and more people showed up, and over the day the atmosphere turned festive. Some understanding was on its way, at last. Late afternoon Viktor lit the barbecue. People clinked glasses. They slugged back the beer and wine. Surely we were on our way now?

Compliments were paid to Bill Francis and Uncle Warwick. Bill with his quiet humility directed all the praise to the strangers. They did not say much at all but looked on as if none of this concerned them and was—how shall I put this?—of passing interest, as if they were casual strollers who had stumbled upon the scene.

In any case, for now their apartness did not matter, caught up as we were in a mood for celebration.

As the evening shadows filled the backyard everyone was

invited to file inside the scaled-up thing which, in our minds, had come to resemble a cage.

Uncle Warwick began squawking like a parrot, then everyone was making bird noises—whistling and hooting and squawking at one another and up at the dusk, where a line of geese flew by, uninterested in the human racket below.

Someone fired an imaginary gun and Viktor, decently, tumbled to the ground. Everyone cheered. Then Mr Fish pretended to reel the kitchenhand back up to his feet, whereupon a second shot rang out and to general cheering Viktor promptly fell down dead again.

What an occasion it was. Dawn whispered in Warwick's ear, and my uncle roared. 'Chicken kebabs this way!'

The last of the sun went down and the air turned cold. People drifted indoors, some of them to the bar, while the locals carried on home.

A few stragglers warmed themselves over the embers of the barbecue, then they disappeared too.

From upstairs, where I'd come to close the windows, the air in the backyard still had a shouted-in quality. By now it was near dark. I would have said the cage was empty. But then a voice laughed out loud. It was the older stranger. He was laughing at himself. Now the other one made the same mistake and walked into the mesh on the opposite side of the cage.

It was funny the first time, and it was hard not to smile. But the second and third times there was no laughter from below. The strangers hurried to different sides of the cage. They were like moths, batting into the sides of the mesh. Their shadows, livelier now, more urgent, split off to try different angles. Each time the cage rebuffed their attempts to be free of it. The gate rattled on its hinges. Now the strangers became angry. Each accused the other of closing the gate behind himself. They began to cry out for help. Politely at first, as if embarrassed by their situation.

I ran off to find Uncle Warwick, and intercepted him coming out of the gents off the bar, buttoning up his flies. He was glowing with sunburn and alcohol.

He listened without any sign of surprise or concern. His eyes grew large and still, and then they slid away from mine.

The key, he said. I'd better ring Bill.

I didn't wait. I hurried through the dining room to the porch outside.

The strangers were still looking up to where they expected help to appear. Light from the upstairs windows lit their faces. Just their lit faces floating on the night.

From the porch I called out, 'Please. Hang in there. Help is on its way!'

But night continued to fall.

8

I could not sleep for knowing the strangers were out in the backyard, inside that wire thing. It was dark so I couldn't see, but presumably they had made beds on the ground. To have a mattress, to be this warm was disgusting. I thought, I can't be alone in feeling this. But a stillness, rather than any urgency, pressed down from above.

Before switching out the light I picked up the clarinet, as is my habit—a couple of bars before sleep. But playing it felt wrong. A note from a clarinet would sound casually indifferent. The strangers would hear it and think the worst. Then someone in the hotel loudly blew their nose and I wondered if the strangers would give up all hope at hearing themselves drift away from the thoughts of others.

I woke soon after dawn, with a dreadful feeling that I was late. I might have missed my bus or train or the opportunity to escape.

There was 'the thing'. Even more surprising than the day before when it had magically changed from an idea into an object.

The two strangers lay on the ground, curled around one another. The younger one with his arm flung out, his head rested on his shoulder.

The sky in the east turned lighter and as the sun caught the top of the cage the backyard reinstated itself. The high brick wall, a narrow beard of ivy, the garden swing, the rooftops beyond of shops and houses, packed in a cluster, lifting out of the night.

To my right the door onto the porch opened, and I ducked my head inside the window. I felt caught out. Discretion is everything in a hotel. You learn to look away. A guest must never see the hand that picks up the crumb that has fallen from her table. A moment later Dawn's legs passed by. I waited, then pulled back the curtain. Her flimsy dressing gown looked unsuited to the haste with which she crossed the wet grass.

The younger stranger sat up and rubbed his eyes. The older one rolled onto his hands and knees, and stayed like that.

Dawn started off with a heartfelt apology. She was ashamed at what had happened—a silly mistake, but then she stopped to concentrate on the older stranger. She said she couldn't address him like that—when he was on all fours.

By way of reply, the stranger mustered himself, walked his hands towards his knees, and rose stiffly.

Now is there anything you need? Dawn asked. A pot of tea? Scrambled eggs? Toast?

The older one gazed at her with a face of pure misery.

Yes, dear lady. If you could find a short-handled spade and a bucket with some sawdust or dirt…and if it is not too much to ask then some toilet paper would be appreciated too.

And he shouted after her—Please hurry!

He looked miserable as he paced the cage. His hands clutched, and unclutched. He stared up at the windows, and at the locked gate of the cage. Shook his head and paced some more.

The door from the dining room opened and I retreated behind the curtain until Dawn's shadow passed.

The spade fitted through one of those irregular holes in the cage—but the bucket wouldn't fit. The younger stranger grit his teeth and tried to pull the mesh apart. He soon gave up— the mesh has a wire component that won't break or tear—and so he took the spade and, on the far side of the cage, he began to dig with some speed. The other one fidgeted with his trouser string. His trousers were around his ankles and his white doughy old-man's bum didn't know what to do with itself. His hands cupped each cheek. The roll of toilet paper was thrown through the hole—then Dawn fled, holding her dressing gown together. She disappeared inside. At the sound of her running up the stairs, I went back to the window.

The younger one finished digging and threw down the spade; he took himself off to the side nearest my window where he stood, his face pressed to the mesh, eyes closed.

The shitting one called out to him 'to sing'. The younger one's face screwed up. He seemed reluctant, or unable to.

Since the clarinet was within handy reach I thought I could help out. I played until…well, until I thought sufficient time had passed. And when I checked at the window the stranger was fastening his trousers. He pulled the string, reached for the spade and began spreading the clean soil.

Word quickly got around, and all day visitors arrived with parcels of food. Our neighbours brought cakes, lasagne covered in foil, still warm. Apples. Pears. Some thought to bring toothbrushes. All of it was delivered through the same feeding hole. We would have dashed upstairs for their belongings had they any. Someone brought boxes of tissues. We should have thought of that. The most obvious things skipped our minds at this point.

Gifts piled up in the cage. A day later, the undisturbed pile was a discouraging sight to those arriving with more.

The older one said to accept the gifts would be to accept the prospect of a longer stay, and that, he said, they did not wish to encourage.

In Bill's plane, we had flown from one set of ranges to the other—the long river valley below holding the bright shadow of our passing. It was beautiful to see the one thing trace a pattern on the other, even though no one would have said they were connected.

Over scrub and under cloud our shadow disappeared, and the sound of the engine filled our ears, so that it felt as though we were inside something that moved and roared on our behalf. Then the sun reappeared and the shadow of the plane landed on the flat surface of the river.

It began to feel as though the river was waiting for us. And trusted us to return. It was just a matter of clear light returning to the skies, then catching hold of something before it quickly vanished.

The Trust was Bill's idea. He said the situation needed to be administered, and that the strangers' wellbeing needed to be managed. At the same time, he felt, there would be plenty of opportunities to glean information.

There was that photograph. Bill reminded us. Boxing Day at the beach. A woman, middle-aged, in a bikini is bending down to examine something of interest in the sand. Over her shoulder a huge and fearsome wave gathers. There is nothing but wet sand and the beachcombing woman with her back turned to the event that will in the next few seconds sweep her away.

Bill's point—imagine if a Trust was already in place. It might see what the beachcombing woman couldn't. It might have shouted out a warning.

Bill would not nominate himself for the Trust. He felt people such as ourselves were needed. We were the ones most affected by what sat in our midst. It made sense. And that, too, was one of the tasks of the Trust: to make sense.

The well regarded Mr Bennett was the obvious choice for chair. The engineer's face is a trusted one. His large nose, round clear blue eyes and steady as she goes line of mouth are among the many reasons he would be a popular choice for mayor. Though he has never run—humility being one of his other strengths. He is also tall. His shirt sits tidily on the points of his shoulders and he holds the other's eye when he speaks. They say people would happily jump off a cliff if he were to recommend it.

To the faces pressed against the cage mesh he explained the problem. One, the mysterious whereabouts of the key. Just one of those crazy things. In the space of a few days it had gone missing. Where hadn't they looked? In this cupboard, under that book, in that pocket, under that teacup.

That was the easier bit to share with the two faces peering back at him. Now, for the more difficult matter. Mr Bennett looked troubled. It clearly pained him to say it.

He told the strangers of his reluctance to use a welding torch on the padlock. It was not the kind that would bend to the will of a hot flame. As for smashing the cage walls down, that, he explained, was out of the question since 'the thing' was an elaboration of their own making. The Trustees were loathe to destroy property, intellectual or otherwise, that belonged to the strangers. It was not how things were done.

Furthermore, as some of the Trustees had argued, one or two quite testily, its destruction would represent the worst of transactions—the strangers' freedom in exchange for our chance to see how the world might end. The Trust, in other words, was invested in their experience.

The strangers did not speak. It was as though they were still listening to what they had just heard.

Still, we wanted the strangers to be happy. And what drove us as well, I think, was a wish to be liked.

The strangers were fed and watered. As soon as Viktor or I arrived with a tray the strangers would move towards the feeding hole. We looked after their needs as best we could.

Dawn passed through a vase of marigolds. The older stranger received them graciously, but the next morning the vase lay in the dirt, the flowers discarded, some of them trampled.

Towards the end of the school week, Katie's class filed into the backyard. She had passed on a note from me to her teacher recommending that the class come shortly before midday. The strangers are usually through their toilet by then. Although, clearly, the children had been told what they might see, if they were lucky, because as soon as they arrived they darted to the chewed-up end of the cage. One boy held his nose and giggled. Then Miss Kidson arranged them in three lines and they sang *Pokarekare Ana*. The strangers clutched at the cage, their fingers buried in the mesh.

The older one's eyes grew moist, his hands gripped the cage. The younger stranger appeared to be lost in thought, or possibly bored.

At the end of the song Katie and her classmates looked up at their teacher, and Miss Kidson redirected their joyful faces to the cage.

The young stranger's applause was reluctant, even the older one's was a bit wooden, but when he saw how hungry the children's faces were, he clapped louder, and for longer.

The serried ranks fell apart. The small boys pushed each other to get closer to the cage.

One boy declared loudly 'a shit smell' and the rest rushed forward sniffing with their sharp little noses.

The strangers waved their arms, as if swatting away flies. The younger one barked a terrible alien noise that thrilled and frightened the boys.

I had to pull one down out of a tree.

9

The clarinet is on the bed. But instead, I reach across for the shaving mirror. My sideburns have grown. I'm not sure it is a concern, but one sideburn has a rust tinge of red I never knew was there. My hair is what used to be called tousled, fair. But now there is this reddishness or rust. A rogue element, as I am coming to regard it. A mystery, at least.

I wonder if this is what my uncle had seen more generally, and quietly marked me down as a work-in-progress, malleable, willing.

A rather insecure feeling had come over me. A provisional idea about my worth.

Sport, you should feel flattered, Uncle Warwick had said. And it was flattering to think of my name passed around by the Trustees, most of whom didn't know me from Adam but were willing to take a punt. And at my age—as Warwick had said.

But what was expected of me? What was I supposed to deliver?

That, we are still to find out, said my uncle.

When does a fish feel itself to be hooked? Is it the moment its mouth opens and closes on the barb? Or earlier—at the sight of the bait? Or does it begin with hidden desire? Desire for what?

To see another as they would never normally allow. To see all those private moments and I don't mean the shitting but that instant when the strangers might have thought they were alone. The public face slips away, the mask lifts. And there they are, their secret selves.

And that, the Trust believes, is our best bet if we are to see all the way back to when they emerged or woke to find their old world gone.

I remember my first morning at the hotel, groggily making my way to the window. And instead of nodding sheep and hills, a garden wall jammed the view. What I expected to see passed in a flash. Impossible to transcribe. Impossible. But it continues—the nagging past does—the rattle of a gate chain, the barking, the distant whine of a farm bike. But I never lurch awake as the strangers do, or pull my feet away from licking flames.

There is a moment when I sense some terrible flashback crossing their faces, usually when they first wake, but I find it impossible to jot down quickly or persuasively enough.

Tonight I cannot sleep. I pull back the curtain and look out. I can make out the strangers on the floor of the cage. They are still, their eyes are closed. But their sides are twitching.

Until now I had never really observed anyone who was unaware they were being watched. I have discovered that the words 'watched' and 'noticed' are not the same as 'observed'.

A man comes to the attention of the police for looking up at the lit window where every night a woman undresses. He has done something no one can accept. The woman's privacy has been violated. Judgment is made in law as well as language. The man is a Peeping Tom.

In public, a glance is fine. You are allowed to notice things. At school, I remember our art teacher encouraging us to look carefully, to make sure we had seen everything we needed to. A casual glance would not do.

With the strangers, I feel as if I am caught between looking at a crisis and wanting to solve it. I am also looking for those things that the strangers might not like others to see. The kind of thing that might say something about who they are and where they are from.

At such moments, I am caught between throwing a lifebelt to the strangers struggling in the sea and waiting to see how they will get on left to their own devices.

I often think of sheep at dusk, and their spectacular single-mindedness—they eat as if in response to a vision of a coming famine. During the day they hardly know what to do with themselves. If they remember to, they nibble grass, but then quickly become bored.

The same applies to the strangers. They look forward to each new day. It may bring their release. And then it passes, and there is another endless night to get through.

At night, sheep will wail, singularly, and in chorus if they are in a pen, each wail sounding more woebegone than the last.

The mutterings of the strangers are not as insistent. Mole will swear and pound the sides of the mesh. Sadder utterances come from Doctor. Suddenly he is someone he wasn't before. He is a sad man.

Is there one stranger we should concentrate our energies on? ask the Trustees.

It is hard to say. Mole is more temperamental, more volatile, more likely to say something he didn't mean to. Doctor will sink into despair, and become a more sodden version of himself, more condensed if anything. With Mole, the doors and shutters fly open, then quickly close again.

'Rose,' I heard him say this afternoon. A girl's name? A girlfriend? A wife? Or a sister? Or a plant?

When I asked him who Rose is, he looked startled, presumably unaware the name had escaped him. He would not tell me, and a smile closed his mouth as he walked across to the log where he sat down, his back turned to me.

One night recently I heard Doctor stir. His voice was wishful and loud—that of an older man whose hearing aid needs to be dialled up.

He was telling Mole about something that happened long ago. A man had fallen down a manhole. He had to wait four days to be rescued. Until then he sat at the bottom of a sewer looking up at a plug of sky that at night became a plate of bright stars. During the day he could hear voices, and he called out to people walking by. Not one heard his cries.

And that is how things are with us, he said. Whatever we say is not heard, or it is taken for a lie.

Now the story of the man trapped in the manhole has morphed into a new nightmare. Doctor arrives back from it yelling up at the lit windows of the hotel. Mole has to gently shove him back down to his bed in the dirt and reassure him— there is no bed of fire. He is not being spit roasted.

In the ledger I write: 'Doctor woke from a nightmare.' I note the hour. Conditions. Stars. Clouds. The falling shadows.

I enjoy making these notes. I have tried to explain the task to Dawn, but I don't think I succeeded. It's one of those things you have to discover on your own. When I began these observations I wrote a sentence across a blank sheet, then sat back, enthralled. It was like encountering the surprise of oneself in a photograph. There I am, I thought. I am in that sentence. The rest of me—my clothes, my name—all that is just cosmetic. Words, on the other hand, speak from a place that cannot be seen. A place beyond the mirror.

Writing something down is a way of stopping time. 'Doctor is sad. He sat with his head in his hands from 10.15pm until 11.17pm.' It turns into a frozen moment for the Trustees to wander around and wonder at, as if Doctor were a statuette in their midst.

My own recurring dream is less startling. I am banging away on my entries. Outside my door, the Trustees wait, their ears bent to the clacking of my keyboard.

Then I stop. Silence. The Trustees straighten up and consult one another. That silence—what is it? It must mean something. Then we listen to each other. Me at my desk. The Trustees outside the door. We share an anxiety that one day I will lower my bucket into a dry well.

What have we learned so far? This is the most persistent question the Trustees ask.

So far, I would say we have learned to overcome our revulsion and shame.

Damp air, a feeling of grievance. A shuffle of oil skins as

they leave the hotel. The Trustees look like shags, eyes ringing private thoughts.

I watch from an upstairs window as their headlights rake the hotel driveway, catch the spooked trees, then vanish into the night.

I often think of the deep silence of the mis-shapen hills, the way they solidify in the summer heat, and when the river dries up and turns white beneath cloudless skies, there is nothing to do but wait out the conditions.

In the morning when I opened the back door small birds flew up from the grass and I could not separate Doctor's expectant look from those of thirsty cattle lined up at the fence.

10

I am tired of telling Katie that I am not their keeper. The kitchenhand's tasks—feeding out, hosing the cage—qualify him more. I will feed out in the morning to help Viktor if there is a breakfast rush. Otherwise my role is simply to observe. I am there—out in the backyard with the strangers—but I am also in this room, behind a pane of glass. We are neighbours, but with a difference. I can see into their lives, but the strangers cannot see into mine.

For a while Katie's avid eyes were taking everything in. But now she is wanting the next thing. Something to eat. Something to look at. Something new and exciting to smell. That shit smell everyone was talking about on their way back to school.

I want to play tennis, she says. Mum said you would teach me.

I very much doubt Dawn has said that, but I have to smile. She is daring me to call her bluff.

In one hand she dangles a child-size tennis racquet, in the other a ratty tennis ball.

What did I say?

You are not the strangers' keeper, she says. Now will you show me?

We will make do with the garden wall for a volley board.

From their log inside the cage, the strangers turn and look our way, and the girl calls out, 'We're going to play tennis.'

We are not going to play tennis. Katie doesn't know how. On a proper tennis court the racquet would be like an oar in her hand. The flight of the tennis ball would outwit both her eye and her racquet.

In front of the garden wall she is impatient to strike the ball. She keeps swishing the air with her racquet and ridiculous ambition. She swings then topples backwards from the momentum.

I snap my fingers for the racquet. And the ball. I tell her not to think of the ball as an object to punish. You simply want to make contact.

I bounce the ball and quietly meet it with the racquet head on the rise. The ball strikes the garden wall and bounces on the grass up into my hand.

Katie demands her turn. As usual she is in too much of a hurry. She hasn't absorbed the lesson at all. She has watched but not in the right way. She wants the wall to return the ball and for it to bounce tidily into her hand, but she doesn't understand her own role in the outcome.

She throws down the ball and swings the racquet at it.

It's a bad shot but also a remarkable one. On the rebound the ball must have struck a stone lying in the grass because it bounces high and drops through one of the gaps in the roof of the cage.

I want my ball! cries the girl.

I have to remind her again. You don't ask like that, remember? Please, can I have my ball?

Mole, moving at his own leisure, bends down to retrieve it. He holds it as he would an apple or a pear; turns it around in his hand, studies it for imperfections.

Now he presents the ball to Doctor. And the older one's face turns into a picture of bristled concentration. He shuffles towards the feeding hole, and holds out the ball to the girl who is jumping up and down on the other side. As she reaches for it he withdraws, holding the ball just beyond her fingertips. Then he turns to me to say he would like a pen and paper, and the possibility of some representation, so that others may hear of their circumstances.

This is one of those incidents I must report to the Trustees. Predictably, my news alters the mood of the meeting. Even Mr Bennett, whose feathers are rarely ruffled, rakes his fingers over his scalp.

But their current circumstances are already known. And, representation? Did he really say that? We are here to help, he begins to say, then stops. Did little Katie get her ball back? he asks.

No. Mole took the ball from Doctor and lobbed it into their shitting area.

Mr Bennett closes his eyes. My uncle swears under his breath.

But there is more. Doctor also asked for a camera.

It is left to Mr Fish to speak to the stunned silence. Well, sure, he says. And what about some photos of the catastrophe. That would be useful.

Then every face at the table looks in the chair's direction for guidance.

Mr Bennett is caught out, his thoughts are still swirling around old news.

We must buy Katie a new tennis ball, he says.

This is one of those instances where I have to ask what to put down in the minutes. Doctor's request, or the proposal to purchase a new tennis ball?

I think a set of tennis balls would be an appropriate gesture, says the chair, and he raises his eye. There is no objection.

I think, however, Mr Bennett continues, you might make a note to the effect of Katie's tennis ball getting soiled. A brief note on how it happened, who was responsible, and that no punitive measures were taken. Something to that effect.

We push on with the agenda. It must be adhered to, like the rules of the road. It is the only way to get anywhere, however tedious.

For this reason I continue to make the same request of the strangers. Each morning I say the same thing. Look, it would be so much easier if you were to give us your names.

Mole closes his eyes and opens his mouth to breathe. We are back to that.

Doctor rises from the log. His approach is wary, like a bear taking its first steps after a long hibernation. The foot with the moccasin trails the booted foot. He makes his assessment from deep inside his whiskered face.

What is your name? he asks.

I am under strict instructions not to provide it. It's a decision of the Trust. A matter of security. What is to stop them from stealing our names and identities further down the track?

You see, says the face behind the mesh. You won't say. Yet you ask us for ours.

Sport, I reply. That's what my uncle calls me.

I have another question, says Doctor.

Yes, I reply. I am here to help as best I can.

The key. Where is it?

I step back from the cage, just in case.

I am sorry, I have no news. Now, is there anything else I can do for you?

It is an unsatisfactory note on which to end.

We talk about their eventual release. What we might do for them. Perhaps by then we will know who they are, in which case their documentation might enable them to stay. If that is what they still wish.

If they decide to move on, we must accept that, says Mr Wooten. We might think about what we can send them off with.

Clothes, says Dawn. She wonders how anyone can wear the same clothes day in, day out, and still retain their human dignity.

And some decent shoes, adds Mr Wooten. Should they choose the road.

The mood of meeting turned melancholic. Later, Viktor stood at the door, a solemn nod for each of the Trustees as they filed out.

So much depends on patience. The strangers are like cattle that dot the hillsides. They are so still they could be mistaken for procelain. Few thoughts to share ever surface on their faces or leave their mouths. If they truly cared about us, they would make more of an effort.

11

Katie and I often visit the zoo. It's not far from the hotel, and it helps me to understand life in the cage. It helps to bring the far near.

At the zoo, the animal returns your stare, or else it pays no attention—it already knows all there is to know about being stared at. The meerkats stand and look interested in everything except the visitor gazing at them.

The strangers will at times adopt the same pose, pretending that they have other business to attend to.

The rhino enclosure is on the left, just inside the gates. That's where we stop first, astonished by a creature that carries all its worldly possessions—its clothes and sleeping mats and rugs. Its ears are soft and pointed like a hare's. Everything else about the creature deflects attention from itself. Except for its suffering eyes. And when I lock eyes with it I see that I am part of its problem—that I am implicated in its suffering.

Around dusk, the place changes hands. The animals sense the change—a cool rush of expectation passes across the zoo as the gates close. The visitors have gone, those easily distracted inspectors of joy strolling along with their ice creams. The lions lift their massive heads, and blink at the dark. The giraffes stretch their canny necks and stick their small heads up between the glittering stars. In the aviary the birds fly in their huddled sleep and crash against the cage. A sickening sound that sets off the chimps. They hoot and whistle. The lions muster up to the bars and roar.

The town lights up. A place of mystery to the zoo's inhabitants. Lights floating on a black night. A kind of sky, or—as it must be supposed—stars fallen to earth.

The animals don't hate us. They alternate between bewilderment and boredom. Take the African raptor—renowned for its 'acrobatic and artistic flight'. It lifts its wings in readiness for take-off. It must know the pointlessness of the exercise by now, yet, to the extent that it can imagine a future for itself, the raptor moves towards it. Its powerful orange talons hold it in place while it energetically beats its wings. Old desire battling it out. Its muscle memory and instinct remain in debt to a world that no longer exists.

Flight is the problem the raptor wakes to each day. It lifts its wings. It catches the air. It waits. The suspense goes on, day after day.

Doctor flew like a demented bird, that afternoon, bashing his head into one side of the cage, then the other. Mole had to restrain him—he threaded his hands up under the older man's armpits and got him to ground where he whispered in his ear until Doctor stopped panting.

Eventually they both got up, Doctor dusted himself off.

A moment later he flew into another rage—flapping his arms, squawking.

Viktor came running out of the kitchen and turned the hose on him.

An hour later it was Mole's turn to be agitated. His hands clawed at the mesh. His bloodshot eyes wished to poison me.

We need towels. Do you understand?

12

The Indian summer continues, thank goodness. A last hooray when the sun gives its all before fading into memory.

The upstairs windows have been left open. The strangers gaze up at their source of shade. The cage offers no protection, and they enter each dusk with new bands of sunburn.

Lately I've noticed them rubbing dirt on their skin. This is Doctor's initiative. I've heard him say that they must forget it is dirt. In any event, they are only rubbing onto their skins what they themselves will eventually become. Their immune systems, Doctor believes, are all the stronger for their life outdoors, and after all, dirt has been man's companion far longer than has soap.

Humidity is the worst. Their reeking clothes turn into cardboard. They sit on the log, listless in the heavy air. The trick, it would appear, is not to move.

Visitors have come to see the strangers. Why are they just sitting there?

The strangers close their eyes and lower their heads. It is the only way they know to remove themselves.

A few fat raindrops splatter on the dirt. The breeze is from the west. Two or three drops fall onto my windowsill.

It is hard to pick up the strangers' conversation when rain is falling. Their words are dragged under, especially those of Mole who is softly spoken.

Whenever it rains the strangers pace. They do it, I imagine, to alleviate feelings of helplessness. Rain is falling and they can do nothing to prevent it. But they are not human gutters. Nor do they wish to be cooperative like grass or submissive like mud, and so they pace.

They pace until one or the other can no longer be bothered, or is exhausted, Doctor it usually is, long after the rain has matted his hair.

Uncle Warwick cheerfully reminds us that the strangers are used to inclement weather. In addition, they have shown themselves to be remarkably adaptable. Doctor, whose table manners no one could possibly question, has shown himself also quite capable of shitting in public.

They have their coping strategies. That's the main point I wish to make to the Trustees. We would turn into sodden paper out there. But some sort of defiant attitude keeps the weather from overwhelming them.

I remember my parents planting a banana tree at one end of what we called 'the farmhouse', a grey cross-eyed timber dwelling saddled with all the gloom of those who had suffered its leaking roof and draughty windows. Planting a banana tree seemed such a wild thing to do. As though we were in the Bahamas instead of these bare hills broken by erosion and sheep shit. We didn't know this country. We were plot gardeners, suburban in outlook and experience. Still, we thought the soil would bend to our will, and so Dad put the banana tree at the north end of the house. Its leaves were glossy and hopeful. We laughed at Dad's enthusiasm. He didn't care what anyone thought. He was planting a banana tree. He seemed to think conviction alone would make it work.

I think of that banana tree whenever I listen to the Trustees speak brightly of the day when there will be no cage, or need for one. The catastrophe will be known. Thanks to the strangers coming to their senses and making an effort to cooperate.

But, for now, the strangers resist our questions.

If they were still homeless and wandering we might know what to make of them. We would feel we knew *that* story. But the strangers look a bit like us—this makes their silence all the more disturbing. Some of the Trustees are beginning to wonder if they actually mean us harm. Why else would they remain silent? For what other reason are they so unyielding?

In their first days of captivity they rushed back and forth across the cage in a panic. Bashing themselves against the mesh. The younger one scraped his nose. When he wiped it, the blood spread across his face, and we all thought, briefly and inescapably, thank God he's inside the cage. The blood and the wild eyes and that crazy mane of hair.

In his charge across the cage, Doctor went more slowly, like an old-fashioned cab, holding up his hands to appeal their circumstances. It became irritating to hear the same thing yelled up at our windows.

Then night removed them from view and we didn't have to think about them until the next day.

There has been more rain. Doctor could just as easily step around the puddles. Instead he splashes through them. Back and forth he goes—water flying up around his ankles—and, with more and more disregard like the same point of an argument returned to over and over again.

Rain. A light drizzle. The birds clutching their roosts fall silent.

Whenever I walk past the people sleeping rough outside the zoo, their eyes lift. They look to see if I think the worst of them, living as they do. As if they are victims of an uncharitable thought. One option is to pretend they are not there. But then they register a new grievance. I have made them invisible.

Today at the zoo, the Indian rhino would not stop looking at us. Katie was embarrassed by its attention.

Make it look away, she said. Make it look away. Then, I'm not looking at it until it stops.

She peeped between her hands.

Stop it! She shouted at the rhinoceros.

She covered up her face, then peeped—Piss off! she shouted.

Hey, enough of that. Look where you are, I said.

Two women in wheelchairs with oxygen tubes into their noses were also looking at the Indian rhinoceros, but with such intent I don't think they heard the lively girl beside them. Their caregivers didn't notice either. They played on their phones.

Let's wander over to the elephants, shall we?

I have been reading a story to Katie about a time when the elephant ruled the world. Several thousand years ago a man in Africa dipped his finger into ochre and painted the world view of the elephant onto a cave wall. In the picture-book illustration the elephant's large eye hovers over the animal kingdom. Thick hide like castle walls. Around its thundering hooves, humans in flight.

A man might slip his head inside a mask of an elephant. Since to be like an elephant was to know unrivalled power.

At the zoo, we see only our differences. That is not the case with the strangers. Visitors see themselves—as they imagine they would be—after a disaster. But what happened? That is what everyone wishes to know. And, how the steps taken might be avoided in the future.

This afternoon, while sitting on the first-floor toilet, I thought, since I'm here I might just jump up on the seat and check the cage. From the small window above the cistern it looked like Viktor's tea strainer. Both strangers lay on the floor, in filth.

It was as if I were flying over the backyard in Bill Francis's plane. The vast spread of the world could be taken in at a glance. That's how it was looking down at the cage. The strangers occupy a more intimate space than any of us can imagine.

Take the selective way Mole will walk to a particular point and lightly push against the mesh—it's as if some amazing new idea has taken root. Now it is just a matter of finding the right square of mesh and lightly pressing on it and they will walk out of there.

Mole holds out his arms. He feels for the place. He looks like a man trying to fit a window in a frame. Or, I suppose, in his case, lift it out.

But how different is that from the raptor as it raises its wings?

The air smells feathery. The skies pass over its meshed ceiling.

I have learned to look from the back. It is as if I am not there, and the Trust is looking through me. If I were to employ my own eye only, I imagine I would feel horror and shame, and the window I wish to be would become clouded and impossible for the Trustees to see clearly through. I am quite sure of this. The moment I wake, my first thought is to wonder if they are awake and, if so, what they are doing.

Soon after the news of the car crash did the rounds, people looked at me in the street and I could see them thinking, it's him, it's that kid. To get through the moment I had to pretend I hadn't seen them, that I hadn't noticed a thing. I had to be like the animals in the zoo and pretend they were invisible.

It is not quite like that with the strangers. They are interested, and curious. Increasingly I feel we are a mystery to them.

Are they sentient in all the usual ways? ask the Trustees.

I will say this. They hear fantastically well. A zip on a visitor's handbag and their heads turn. Perhaps it is the woman from the agency.

Every female visitor is met in the same hopeful way. It's as if at last their prayers have been answered. They rise from the log and approach the mesh with a smile.

It amuses some that the strangers should be so sure about what is, in fact, speculation.

The Trustees have no idea what the woman from the agency looks like either. A visit has been promised? None of the Trustees know where they got that idea from—a woman in a hard hat, the strangers claim. Accustomed to trouble spots, civil war, strife, humans behaving badly.

But back to their hearing...The screech of a car's brakes from the other side of the hotel, for example—when they hear something they cannot see, their eyes gain in intensity, their skin tightens.

They are back out there, in the world, until a leaf drops through the mesh and their attention is returned to the dirt inside the cage.

A camera flash, or a child pointing, and asking his mother, 'Why can't they talk?' and all hope recedes. It is not the woman from the agency after all.

Their bashful faces retreat. They vanish back inside themselves. They present their skins, their cloaks of rags. They absorb the probing eyes of the crowd. They absorb.

Do they get bored? ask the Trustees.

They have each other, I remind them, and they have their conundrum, that knot that cannot be untied.

If they sit for too long they become melancholic.

It can happen with pets. As a child, I kept guinea pigs. I loved their little pink noses. I had rabbits too. One ended up in the jaws of a cat. Another soared over the roof in the talons of a hawk.

One never anticipates the end until it arrives in all its surprising ways.

13

My uncle was happy. It was like a nice blast of cleansing summer air through the hotel. The dining room was full. The cash register ringing. Bookings were high. He and Dawn were busy, dashing up and down the stairs. And it was left to me and Viktor to look after the strangers.

Crowd numbers vary. Weekends are busy. Weekdays not so much. Autumnal sunshine, and everyone turns out—filing through the hotel, pushing strollers. Or they swing themselves along on canes. No one is too young or too old.

On busy days the strangers imagine they are back in our world. Doctor more so. He speaks intelligently. Perhaps too intelligently, and too purposefully, for some.

A smiling face will encourage him up from the log. He's warmed to something that we suspect he recognises from his old life, the one he says has vanished. He ambles up to the mesh, and nods agreeably, as if to say, 'Look here, I am just like you.' As though this is a chance to remind one and all that they stand beside a mistake—one which needs to be urgently corrected—for the cage holds a face like their own, eyes like theirs, a skin and a bundle of fears and anxieties like their own.

A visitor might react with surprise. There's been a

misunderstanding. His smile wasn't so much for Doctor but his circumstances, a rueful smile for the state of the world, the accident of birth, the hidden trajectories that sets one life apart from another.

The strangers are in the cage—the visitor is not. The boundary could not be any clearer.

Two days ago, a man, irritated by a lack of response, stuck a rake handle through the feeding hole in an attempt to knock the younger stranger from the log. Mole crossed his legs and turned away. This infuriated the visitor all the more. He kept prodding and probing until he was red in the face. Mole continued to sit unconcerned just beyond reach. Then the thrusting and jabbing stopped. The visitor with the rake had seen the hose. I ran out there just in time.

Usually Mole is more effective at shaking off a persistent visitor—he will walk to the middle of the shitting area and stay there.

It's no surprise to see Doctor become the crowd favourite. He is more willing to engage. Doesn't mind having his photograph taken with a visitor. He answers a few questions sincerely. Or else he will step graciously away, shaking his head.

I wish I knew, he will declare. Regrettably, I cannot say.

As a general rule I try not to intervene. It muddies things if I become part of the scene that I am supposed to observe. Warwick says I should try to think of everything that happens in the backyard as if it were happening on a screen.

It's the only way, Sport, he said. You'll figure it out.

This afternoon a small boy climbed onto the roof of the cage. I was of two minds what to do. I should do nothing, according to Uncle Warwick. It turns out he was right.

Doctor stationed himself beneath the boy, and raised his gnarly old hands, but that alarmed the boy, who began to cry. To everyone's surprise it was Mole who came to the rescue. He talked softly to the boy. Talked him across the roof to the far corner and the spread arms of his father who stood in the wheelbarrow Warwick had fetched from the shed.

The situation should have been avoided in the first place. Now the Trustees wonder if the time has come to think about erecting a barrier around the cage. As a health-and-safety measure, it has some support. Though Mr Wooten worries that it will place more distance between us and the strangers. When the whole point of the exercise, ever since the strangers came into our lives, has been to get close enough to win their confidence in order to discover what they know.

I put in the ledger 'No?' with a question mark. I don't like the idea of a barrier, but ultimately it is for the Trustees to decide.

I did point out, however, that visitors like to toss the strangers sweets and nuts. They scrabble around in bags for gifts, cigarettes, apples. Some bring sketchbooks, crayons, charcoal, pencils in all varieties, erasers of all shapes.

The other day each stranger held a sketchbook—their donors implored them to put down some detail from their experience of the catastrophe. The strangers stared at the blank pages until expressions of hopelessness and inadequacy returned to their faces.

At busier times, during the weekends, for example, the Trustees are rostered on to keep an eye on things.

Last Sunday, a woman unwound a scarf from her neck. She

was about to put it into the feeding hole when Mr Byrd, who happened to be on duty, pulled it away.

What if they had hung themselves!

Unnecessary to say so, some Trustees felt afterwards.

A look of wonder and horror entered the woman's eyes.

She wound the scarf back around her neck, then unwound it. She held it up to examine it one last time, and, as she bunched it in her hands, Doctor sank to his knees and made a prayerful plea. Would she not change her mind?

No. She couldn't. She dropped the scarf in the rubbish bin newly installed by the Trust and hurried away, back through the hotel.

14

Complaints have increased. The strangers feather their nest. It is all they show an appetite for, self-interest.

A young man offers them some potato chips. He is obliged to push the bag into the feeding hole and Mole snatches it. He eats each chip with insolent pleasure, refuses to return the bag to the visitor.

A Japanese honeymooning couple set up a tripod. They placed themselves between the camera and the cage. The strangers did their best to upset the shot. They kept shifting to a new place. The groom would not give up, even when the strangers moved themselves to the shitting area. At his wits' end he reached into his pocket and produced two barley sugars. He held one in each hand. The strangers came shyly forward. They accepted the barley sugars. Placed them in their mouths. Their cheeks bulged as if they were each chewing on the buckle of a belt. And then, for once, they did the decent thing and stood behind the couple, shifting the sweets inside their cheeks for the photograph to be taken.

I felt relieved. I suppose this is what parents feel. Or people with dogs that like to shit on a particular lawn. As soon as that house is passed without incident the dog owner looks from the dog to the house and back to the dog with relief.

We have our protocols in place. And, as my uncle says, anyone interested enough to want to do an audit would come away more than satisfied. The system is not the problem, he says. It's the bloody people.

A sign clearly states 'No Photographs'. But people take them anyway. Doctor will sit on the log with his legs crossed as he might on a bench above a riverbank to watch a watery parade of colourful punts.

People don't respect advice. They think it is for others. They give the impression that they are listening, but are too impatient to take in the safety measures included in Uncle Warwick's 'Talk to First-timers' on what to expect and how best to approach the cage.

The visitors race ahead in their excitement. Then, after a few laps of the cage, they become used to the idea of it. Emboldened by the mesh, they begin to strut and beam.

Usually a first-time visitor and the strangers will stare at each other, like children beginning school, each afraid the other will judge them. They want to be liked, if not friends. At other times the cage appears to melt away.

This afternoon a child cried in his stroller, a terrible wail of distress that would not let up. The strangers and the visitors were all turned into pillars of salt until the mother calmed her child down. We unfroze and moved back into our assigned roles, namely those who are there to be looked at and those who had come to look.

In the event of criticism—not enough is being done to secure the strangers' release; they don't have proper bedding, or bathing or toilet facilities—Mr Wooten will adopt a smile that blazes until the complaints run out of air.

Mr Bennett's weakness is his enthusiasm. He tends to rattle on about engineering details—the challenge of building above a septic tank—unaware that interest has slipped away.

The visitors' questions to the strangers are surprisingly alike.

Were there any signs of impending catastrophe?

In the event of the same catastrophe rolling this way should they expect pain?

Can they recall any political rhetoric immediately before the event? Seconds before or after the catastrophe—a gloating? A sign hauled across the sky by a light plane, for example?

Did anything flash across their screens?

What happened to the household pets? Cats. Dogs. Ponies. Canaries. What about their behaviour beforehand? Dogs are well known for their prescience.

Did it hurt? That question again.

The strangers will not say. But isn't their silence an answer of sorts?

Might it be better not to know anything? And to go about our daily lives like lambs gambolling in the dusk, unaware of where the truck will deliver them in the morning?

We cannot see inside another's mind. Or can we?

There is that moment when the strangers wake. They are as they would be at home. They rise to their feet, move to the fridge or the window, reach for a teabag or a shaving brush, and are then abruptly brought to a halt by the cage. Pressed around their eyes is a bruising confusion. They stand mesmerised by their circumstances, where just a moment ago—in their minds at least—they were in their kitchen at home.

Some visitors are thrown into nostalgia. They recall summers past, blue skies, happy families, sun umbrellas, women gliding by, trailing skirts and tastefully looking the other way if an animal happened to defecate.

Unfortunately we cannot guarantee the strangers' behaviour in that regard. They shit when the need takes them.

The stench, at times, drives me from the window and I suck at the basement air like a fish.

For that matter, the strangers cannot predict their own responses. A visitor might remind them of long ago when they were children full of curiosity and mischief. Or a woman in a puffer jacket holding up her phone might remind one of a former lover. He is likely to walk to the mesh and stare, his lips moving in an unintelligible love-struck way.

More than Mole, Doctor is prone to sentimentality, to musing on his childhood. Days of endless summer, picking wild blackberries and running barefoot through the grass.

Running! A thought so surprising to the visitor that she burst out laughing.

Near the exit some visitors search for a pen so they can scribble down their complaints on a slip of hotel stationery. The complaints box, courtesy of the Trust, is near the back door. A visitor might complain that Mole gave him a filthy look. Or that Doctor had asked for a child's chocolate.

The most common complaint is that the visitor was 'looked at'. And the most common question? 'Are the strangers happy?'

Of course they are. Why wouldn't they be? They are out of harm's way. Their meals are taken care of. No longer do they need to forage or risk their skins travelling at night across unfriendly territory.

~

When he eats carrots Doctor will shift his weight onto one side, as though eating the carrots fills one side of him but not the other. His mouth seems to rotate, his belly shakes.

The younger one tends to stand more square on, his weight more evenly distributed, like the more thoughtful and hungry eater he is. He reaches into his pocket and a visitor cries, 'Look! He's eating an apple!' And the spell is broken. Worse, my notes are compromised by what another person has seen and said. It is annoying. But, short of hammering in another notice, there is nothing I can do about it.

The apple did cause some concern. One or two of the Trustees wanted to know how the apple had got inside the cage.

Viktor was marched upstairs to explain. He claimed there were no apples in the hotel at present.

Mr Bennett flicked through his file—everyone waited— then he looked up to remind Viktor that apple pie was on the menu a week ago.

All the apples were used, replied Viktor.

Mr Bennett turned to Mr Hughes, the grocer. How many apples does it take to make an apple pie, Frank?

Dawn got in before him. For goodness sake, it depends on how big a pie. This is ridiculous. What harm is an apple?

That we have yet to find out, fortunately, replied Mr Bennett.

After clearing my throat to get everyone's attention, I said it was possible, even likely, that a visitor had given the strangers an apple each.

Viktor thanked me later, with macaroons. We sat on the swing in the backyard eating them out of the packet.

The strangers sat on the log with their heads hanging down.

How much longer do you reckon? asked Viktor.

Longer what?

Incarcerated, he said.

They are not incarcerated, they are temporarily caged.

And the difference?

Incarcerated implies we put them in the cage. When, in fact, as you well know, Viktor, they put themselves there. I returned to the macaroon. I crunched my way through it, bulldozing my way through a forest of rage that Viktor had planted.

I did pass on Viktor's comment to Uncle Warwick, who I met coming down the stairs. He looked stunned.

'Incarcerated? Did he really say that?'

At the next meeting of the Trust, Uncle Warwick repeated the kitchenhand's comment, which produced some nervous twitters around the table.

Who are we incarcerating? asked the chair, his arms folded across his chest. He smiled hard. If we had names we could justifiably say that 'John' or 'Vassily' or whoever is inside the cage. But they have no names. No ID. No papers. Nothing.

Silence.

He continued. We did not ask them to come here. We did not say, *You may pitch your tent here.*

I was scribbling all this down as fast as I could—to capture, if I could, this new tone which seemed to be out to persuade the very air we breathed.

I caught up, then stopped to meet Mr Bennett's eye. He nodded.

Does it matter that they don't have IDs? I asked. After all, ghosts don't urinate or defecate. And so, I guess they are someone.

Mr Bennett got up and walked to the window. Some moved their chairs out, believing as I did that he was about to open the curtain. But Mr Bennett changed his mind and came back to the table.

What else? he asked.

The strangers are nocturnal, I said. In the sense they are barely there in daylight, but luminously present when everybody else is tucked up in bed.

It can be quite late at night as I sit by my open window to jot down what I hear from the cage. I have to write quickly and in two columns to indicate who has said what. But some of the sounds can't be transcribed.

Weeping, for example. I am pretty sure it was Doctor. But to write 'he wept' seems inadequate. Like saying 'they arrived' and being satisfied with that, instead of asking why.

Something must have prompted the weeping, but what? I find it impossible to say. And, for that matter, what to make of the surprisingly tender and consoling sound of Mole? What to say about this?

I put my pen down. Some moments, I have decided (without wider consultation), deserve their privacy.

Besides, so far our awareness of their misery has not led to anything changing. What is the point of sympathy that does not produce a change of circumstance?

Quite apart from all that, if I dash out there and offer sympathy the moment will lose its authenticity. It will become confused with my reason for dashing out there.

The strangers cannot explain, and I cannot offer them anything. What we are left with is a cage wall between us.

People in crowds stare unabashed. Sometimes the strangers are driven into the recesses of the cage.

The canny visitor waits until feeding out. Then the strangers emerge, resentful of their appetites. They crouch down to take the corn cobs from me.

A young woman with olive eyes asks me if she may speak to the strangers.

What would you like to say? I ask.

It is none of my business, but I suggest a few talking points. Try to look past their filth, I add. At this time of year, apart from one hour mid-morning, their shitting area is in shade.

The woman is short. When she looks up at me, I recognise the problem. I am a difficult train conductor taking issue with the particulars of her ticket.

She is shy. Her arms are bare. Drifts of dark hair cover her forearms, her eyebrows are thick and dark. She wears blue jeans, casual leather shoes, a white blouse. The strap of a red clutch is wound around her wrist. Her arms are folded, and she shifts from side to side. Her eyes have stopped seeking. They are still and patient.

Mole emerges. He raises a hand to the blinding light, his face pale from shit inhalation.

The woman steps closer. She addresses him in Spanish. Is it Spanish?

The stranger crawls nearer.

She pushes herself forward. An imagined barrier bites her

stomach. She leans over further.

The stranger's pebbled face is now pressed into the mesh.

The two cannot get any closer. The woman reaches into her red clutch. Pulls out a tiny dictionary, a miniature glossary of understanding.

When she speaks, the words are rushed, foreign.

Doctor hurries from the shitting area. This is the most excited I have seen him. He gabbles away, then stops.

He starts again, and stops.

Doubt enters his face.

Now, disappointment.

Why hasn't the woman replied?

She is tearing through the tiny pages. She has lost her place. Her eyes squint at the tiny print. She shakes. She turns the pages of the dictionary.

Doctor drops his head.

Mole steps back from the mesh.

And then, all at once, the two of them squawk at the woman.

She is not who they took her to be. She is not the woman from the agency.

Lines of frustration deepen across Doctor's forehead and the points of Mole's eyes harden.

The woman produces a camera. There is a barrage of flashes and the strangers shrink back to the shitting area.

A silence that has the temperament of a siege falls over the cage.

It is astonishing how still they can be. Some visitors—well, children mostly—will hold their breath to see if they can make themselves as still. Some are reminded of stuffed owls.

15

At the zoo there is the same sense of a performance. The elephants stand there while their life habits are listed by the keeper through a loudspeaker. Then, as the small crowd drifts away, the keeper reaches into his pocket for the peanuts that the elephants have been waiting for.

Today, I listened to a warbler. It doesn't have the loudest of voices, but perhaps that is what singled it out among the shrieks and roars. I listened to it for some time, and soon I heard it as if it were the loudest. But were the Trustees to ask me to reproduce the sound I doubt I could. All I would be able to say is that I remember the sound made by the warbler.

This is the nature of the bind we are in with the strangers. They have come through a devastating event. But to say more than that is impossible for them.

I find it just as hard to say anything useful whenever Dawn puts on a caring smile to ask me how I am getting on? It is a different question, but one aimed at that same unanswerable space.

Dawn keeps an eye on me. She watches me the way she watches the kettle. I wonder what she says to my uncle. How much of what she tells him would I recognise as me.

~

These days on my way to the zoo, I find myself assessing everything as if I were at the window. The streets are now the backyard. And I reach for my notebook, and make my lists.

This morning—the smell of dog.

A gritty metallic smell of unwashed clothing, jeans stiff with dirt, socks not washed since they left God only knows where.

Red skin on swollen cheeks.

Eyes buried in sickly folds of skin.

An arm flung among the filth of cigarette butts, spilt grog, empties, pizza cartons, cheese that is yellow and hard.

A chubby palm still clutching at what must have been a good idea at the time.

Missing daughters in torn jeans and metal studs.

The roar of the traffic.

A wristwatch (that's unusual).

Grey stubble (usual), a neat trim (unusual).

One of the street people wakes. His eye opens. Apricot-coloured face.

A man plunges his head inside an orange rubbish bin. He is up to his armpits, searching and feeling around with his eyes. What of his old life can he find? When did he leave it all behind? Was he aware of the moment of loss as it happened?

I could ask the foraging man. But that would shrink the distance I've established. It would bring me too close. I would become part of what I am observing.

There is an art to looking, and an art of being looked at.

The strangers have perfected the latter.

They look up, avert their eyes, and look down again.

I might as well not be there.

Where is *there*, for the strangers? If I look quickly, I see palm trees, a sweep of beach, the teeming tidal flats. I am there—almost. In some kind of make-believe place. Then they look up, and it has gone. In its place is the mud of the cage, the lived-in air, the barkless skin of the log that I see is beginning to shine.

Last night, sitting on the windowsill listening to Mole's attempts to console Doctor, I began to sob. I could not stop sobbing. My eyes filled with tears until I could not see the ruled lines in the ledger open on my knee.

Then a voice spoke in the dark.

Sport. Can you hear me?

It was Mole.

Sport, he said. You are not like them.

I closed the window—ashamed to know I'd been heard.

In the morning, even though he was standing over three spitting frying pans, I asked Viktor to do the feeding out. I could not face Mole.

The toaster popped up. Uncle Warwick juggled a slice of toast and it fell onto the floor. He picked it up, scraped the burnt bits off with a knife and added it to the pile. No eggs this morning. There was a run on them at breakfast.

This perplexing situation might have continued but for a remarkable observation made by my uncle.

'We know history has occurred even if the details are unclear to us. We still know that something happened.'

A number of Trustees looked up. The nods continued around the table. Something had happened. We needed to recognise that something had happened.

Something needed to be constructed. A memorial.

When Uncle Warwick finished, I could have sworn I could hear the quiet insistence of Bill Francis.

The backyard of the hotel was the obvious place. Public land for a memorial that could not identify what was being remembered might be too much to ask.

Once the strangers had got on their way, the memorial would take their place. People would gather here—preferably after a lunch in the hotel—and point to the memorial as an expression of what they themselves could not describe.

A photo would allow them to say, 'Here I am, in the lap of history.'

Uncle Warwick thought it an attractive idea. It meant the hotel would also by proxy be in the lap of history. Its cash registers ringing.

Discussion now shifted to where exactly in the backyard the memorial should be erected.

On this matter, Mr Wooten was a step ahead of everyone. He felt the memorial should take exactly the same shape and character of the conundrum, and that too made sense.

I assumed the memorial would be built alongside the cage. Mr Bennett put his oar in to scupper that idea.

A pile of rocks could not hope to achieve the same shape without sophisticated engineering input and considerable extra expense.

Why not build, stone by stone, rock by rock, an outer layer that would fit over the existing cage?

What about the strangers?

Extra protection in winter, increased privacy, greater opportunity for domesticity.

The Trustees kept coming up with the advantages. By now everyone was convinced.

Until Dawn said, No. What I mean is, what about the strangers? What do we tell them?

We don't *tell* them anything, replied Warwick. We involve them. We invite them to come up with the words for the memorial. We engrave their description of the catastrophe on a plaque.

Who could argue with that?

After all, what words did they know that we did not? What might they say that we could not understand?

By words, the Trustees meant familiar ones—cows, cloud, wind, rain, fence-lines, sky, recession, roads to nowhere.

The exercise seemed so straightforward. To address the catastrophe so that it would know itself by name.

The next day, in my lunchbreak, my uncle came down to my room for a rare visit. I thought he had a job lined up for me. I put down the clarinet, stood up from the bed and waited for the instruction.

He slouched in the doorway, and he looked around the room until he found what he was after.

A photo of Mum and Dad, it turned out. They are sitting on the deck at home, smiling—at least, Mum is. Dad is squinting back from under the shade of his hand.

Uncle Warwick reached for the photo. In his hands, my parents looked happy with their lives, with the sun-saturated moment. My father used to shave only once every two or three days, but in that photo his face is smooth. He looks younger than I remember him, and more content. My mother who never liked having her photo taken has made an exception because it is her birthday. Sitting together on the splintered deck at the front of the house, they look less like someone's parents, more themselves, as people I never knew, lovers I suppose, friends to start with, as shy as deer, exchanging light glances. It is late January, that time of year when everything stops growing, and even time stops still. Nights arrive reluctantly. Here, in the photo, are my parents as my uncle had never seen them.

Warwick stared at the photo in his hand. He seemed to see his brother for the first time. We should get it framed, he said. It's the only way to look after it.

16

One afternoon a truck reversed up the drive in front of the hotel. Ten tonnes of rock and stones slid down in a steady drumming pour, then a succession of thuds and then a sound of skittles as stones landed between rocks and rock clattered against stone.

Stones only look irregular by themselves. In the company of other similarly shaped stones and boulders these irregularities disappear and you stop seeing what caught your eye in the first place. And, on a dry-stone wall, as I was to learn, one irregularity can perfectly accommodate another.

There is only one wheelbarrow. I fill it with the larger rocks, then add smaller ones and stones, and cart them load by load around the side of the hotel to the backyard.

The rocks are a surprise to the strangers, even though they must have heard the truck release its load. Doctor sits up straighter, his head turned. I tip up the wheelbarrow. And Doctor's interest shifts as I drag a large rock from the pile. Mole squats and shits. My lungs want to dig deeper with the hard work but I can't let that shit smell crawl down my throat.

There is no pane of glass between us. We are in the same

space. And it is not pleasant. It is hard to look without prejudice. I don't know what I would see if I were to empty my eye of thought.

Stone cannot speak of all the time it has accrued. It cannot speak of weather. Stone cannot look back or look ahead.

But it does collect the heat of the day, which is why at night the strangers have taken to snuggling up against the far side of the cage where the wall, so far, is at its highest.

They watch me work and look amused.

What are you building? asks Doctor, Mole beside him.

I've kept my distance ever since the night the strangers heard me sobbing. They would want to know the reason for it, and quite honestly I would not know what to say. And that other phrase Mole used—*You are not like them*—I don't want to think about it, or know what he meant.

I carry on, sweat dripping onto the stone. The work is methodical and repetitive. But there is the satisfaction of seeing progress made with every stone I place. And, the faster the better. As soon as the memorial is finished, it will be up to the strangers to solve the problem they have created for themselves. Then they can get on their way.

Doctor tries again.

Are you planning to entomb us? Is it a tomb you are building?

I push a heavier rock into place, and a lightness returns to my shoulders.

Sheep, says the younger one. *Baaa. Baaa.*

It is the first bit of information I have had to offer the Trustees in days.

Sheep? asked Uncle Warwick. Is that all he said? Sheep?

Yes, I said.

What can it mean?

Probably just that. Mole has some experience of sheep. In his other life, I mean.

And that's all? Uncle Warwick waited.

Well, Doctor asked again if there had been any news.

And? Did you answer?

I had to stop and think if there was a reason why I shouldn't.

And?

I decided there wasn't.

And?

I said, No.

As the stone wall rises, the world rolls on, but without the strangers.

Viktor pushes corn cobs through the feeding hole.

They do not move.

The woman in the hat? asks Doctor.

Viktor turns away and hurries back to the hotel with the slops pail.

Out in the street, children roar and shriek. Dusk smells of wood smoke. Cars passing the hotel slow to stare. Outside the shops, across the road from the hotel, I often catch a face caught in a blaze of gossip. Nobodies, says my uncle. He resents them all. Everyone is an expert until they are asked to get involved.

In the street, people I don't know look at me, then they look away.

Some visitors of late have commented on the haunted appearance of the strangers. But that is not a criticism since the observation meets their expectations. A haunted appearance is what might be expected from survivors of a catastrophe.

Their clothes add to the effect. Trousers that are too short on Mole. The shirt on Doctor balloons but he is made pigeon-chested by the dusty black suit jacket.

The visitors go on staring, unaware of their faces settling into judgment. They—the strangers—are not like them.

An elderly woman in a woollen hat turned up one day last week. She insisted she knew them. She said she had been clipping her hedge when the strangers passed.

Every morning she visits the backyard to count the eyes, mouths and ears of the strangers. She shouts at Doctor to remove his moccasin. She wants to count his toes. Then, she starts over. She has dementia. Patterned behaviour is essential to her. She is never satisfied with what she has seen the day before. She needs to see it again, and again.

The strangers are used to her. They have dealt with officials, they know her kind, they say.

Late in the day Doctor will sit on the log, waggling his booted foot and mumbling nonsense. I try to record his words, and have come up with a special notation. Slurred lines, trembling lines, and sharper incisions, vertical and horizontal movements.

There is a pattern, but its meaning is as far away as ever.

The mouth of the younger one is prone to hang open. But then without warning it will snap shut and he will rise to his feet in a threatening way.

Someone has taken Doctor's photo without asking permission. He doesn't care. In fact he will often pose for a photo. Make his back straighter and lengthen his neck to suggest a seventeenth-century Venetian nobleman.

On the right side of his face between the corner of his eye and the nose bone is a small blossom—rosacea. If he is sitting on the log he will turn his head to offer the camera his left profile.

He is often caught out by a phone turned to video. He will hold himself for the customary length of time required to take a photo before the Venetian Count slumps back to the familiar dumpy dimensions of the stranger. The transformation on film appears as a slow convulsion.

I wish to say something more about Mole. Something about his character.

I am finding it hard to put behind me the incident all those weeks ago where he placed his foot on my wrist.

It was wilful.

Yet the same person is as docile as a child whenever I spoon egg into his mouth.

Is he docile because of the delicacy of the transaction? My hand holding the spoon tends to wobble. Mole is naturally keen to balance the spoon. This will be his only egg for the day.

Sometimes Doctor will put on a heavily accented voice to distract the visitor away from his true self, the way a bird will drag its wing to draw a predator away from its nest.

What do the zoo animals think about all day long? What they have lost?

The forest has gone. The great jungle has been bulldozed. Giant trees lie abandoned, like toothpicks.

The parrot may remember what no longer exists. It squawks

to birds that are extinct. Its eye shifts in response to a vanished canopy.

Without the enormous trees to catch it, the mist evaporates, the waterways diminish.

The clouds race on.

The parrot's eye rolls and rolls and nothing catches.

Darkness arrives, lights appear in the outside world. They must wonder if they will ever step another foot in it.

There are noises from the hotel that mark the shift of activity from morning, to afternoon, to night. It is like listening into lives that were once their own.

Doctor sits on the log with his head hanging low. His circling fingers are searching for new entanglement, new expression. Or are his fingers clutching at what is lost?

17

If the strangers truly cared, they would make more of an effort. The observation won't go away, and takes us easily to the next thought. Why do they wish us harm?

Around the table, the Trustees revert to their innocent private selves. They turn back into ordinary men of trade—an engineer, a fruiterer and casual hobbyists—who mean no harm. There is no place on the agenda for their feelings, and that leads them deeper into their wounded selves.

There has been a request for raspberry jam, I note, and look up, ready to be advised.

No. Their decision is unanimous.

I begin to explain that Doctor's sweet tooth is limited to raspberry jam. Mole will eat anything. But I am interrupted by the chair, who is surprised to hear me try to change their minds. He wishes to remind me that the Trust has reached its decision.

However, it is not their job to explain to Doctor that his request has been declined. It is not their job to disappoint.

I wait until after breakfast, a time when Doctor is at his most optimistic. Perhaps the woman in the hat will turn up today.

As soon as I tell him the light in him fades, and his mouth

drops. It makes no sense, unless the Trust's denial is to make him bitter. Why else would they deny him raspberry jam?

I cannot say. My job is to be a pane of glass for the Trustees and strangers to meet on either side.

I could steal some jam for Doctor. But how would he conceal it inside the cage? And, upon its inevitable discovery, the Trustees would ask, 'How did the jam get inside the cage?'

Would you like me to play the Mendelssohn?

Doctor glances up. His mind surges past me. The jam has put him into an agitated state.

Yes, yes, he says. That would be very nice. Thank you.

He places his hand over his heart, and I think he is going to say it. *You are not like them.* But, to my relief, he nods. Thank you.

18

It is black out there in the backyard. The shadows are so dense the strangers can't be told apart, but then one lashes out. That'll be Mole. Contact with the cage wall pulls him from his dream, and he starts bellowing.

They are trapped. There is no way out.

They are locked in.

I pick up my clarinet and play softly. Eventually, a stillness settles over the cage, and the strangers slip from view. They have lain down on the ground to go to sleep.

In the morning all that is forgotten. Mole's nightmare, and my good deed—blasted out of the backyard by the early morning sun and clear skies.

Look, a new day. New prospects.

The woman in the hat, they ask. Is there any news?

Their new questions concern procedure. Why haven't they been processed and put into the correct category?

And, why is it impossible for anyone to see that but for the cage they would be just like anyone else?

But who looks like they do? Unshaven, dressed in rags, stinking of shit? Who grovels like they do? Who cannot say where he is from?

I have shown them pictures of various places. Cities bombed into ruin. Fortresses shattered, sky-gaping apartment blocks.

Mole is first to give up. He returns to the log. Doctor stares a hole through the pictures.

Why do they not try to help themselves? That is the question that preoccupies the Trust.

How to explain this?

Yesterday when Katie and I were at the zoo, a tapir was stripping a branch when suddenly it kicked itself in the nuts. It fled as if flight would take care of the injury. If asked to explain itself, what would the tapir say about how the injury had occurred? It had kicked itself in the nuts. But why? It would not be able to say. It could only point to its bruised nuts and a hoof print in the dirt. It cannot explain why it fled or point to that thing that spooked it.

The strangers speak so infrequently nowadays they might as well be two statues standing in the rain, sword in scabbard, a tilted hat, a prideful eye.

Visitors speak as if they are not there, as if they really are statues standing in the rain.

A cheap white handbag hangs off the arm of the woman with dementia. She believes she has arrived at a wedding. Instead, she is watching Doctor shit.

And so it goes.

The raptor raises its wings. The gazelle stops and stares. The flamingos hop and bounce, but go no further. The great African eagle considers the innards of a white mouse for the fourth time that morning. It sits and waits for its appetite to arrive.

After his ablutions, Doctor's attention shifts to the next task.

He wishes to be useful. He has all the mannerisms of someone used to stoking the faith of others.

He turns this way and that. He strokes his stomach.

Mole paces, varies his stride.

It is as if their past is pulling on their limbs, and eyes. Their mouths shift and set into new lines.

Why do they not speak of loved ones?

I showed Doctor a picture of a city devoured in an inferno, and he raised his hands as if to shield himself from the flames. Then he returned to the log, where he sat, with his hands in his pockets.

Mole has a grip of the wire near the shitting area.

He doesn't like to be seen exercising and will tolerate the shit smell in exchange for the protective shadow at the end of the cage.

The rest of the time he gives the impression of being without a care in the world. I wonder if he led a bohemian life. It is impossible to think of him and Doctor as being from the same tribe.

But on one topic they are in agreement. They take it in turns to say *You are not like them.* Doctor says it with a burning intensity. Mole will set his head on its side, as if he knows and is waiting for me—slowboat—to catch up.

Do you know where the key is? he asks.

No. And it is the honest-to-God answer.

But if you knew?

If I knew, I would be first in line to set you and Doctor free.

He thinks about what he just heard, nods. And I look for another rock to place. I don't look up. I have a horrible feeling that there is a face in the upstairs window, and that somehow

I have let everyone down. I work harder and faster than I need to. And that makes Mole uneasy.

Say it again, he says in that soft imploring way of his. I want to hear you say it.

This morning a new visitor arrived, and Doctor eagerly sidled up. I was working nearby on the memorial walls, but did not feel any need to include myself beyond listening.

Where? he asked the newcomer. Where is the woman from the agency? We were promised a visit from her.

Mole released himself from the bars, and rushed across to the mesh.

She wears a helmet, he said.

So we believe, added Doctor. Do you know such a woman?

The visitor was startled by their questions. The way they talked at him, trying to obtain his interest, implicate him. He stepped back to put himself beyond the striking distance of the strangers.

We are just like you, said Doctor, and the fullness of Mole's grubby face spread across the cage mesh.

We are just like you.

Frustration—it strikes everyone differently.

A child drops its ice cream and Doctor's face will go perfectly still, like the bloated profile of a nobleman on a coin.

Lovers kiss and touch, and the strangers are left to gaze into a playground unavailable to them.

Then they remember their own craving. They remember past joys. And the question springs from happier times. Is there any news?

I shake my head. I shake my head again if I'm not happy with the way I shook it the first time. I try not to let it irritate me.

It requires effort to say No as many times as the question is asked. I try to say it in such a way that does not attack or undermine the question.

19

I squeeze into the back of the car next to Katie and her friend from school, the shit-smelling boy, whose name is Ryan. Out in the country I feel myself begin to relax. Dawn was right to say a change of scene would do us good. The uncomplicated paddocks sprawl away from the road. A patchwork of grazing and arable land. The sky grows larger. It is my old life, and it is taking me back.

We park by a disused shearing shed. From the car Dawn carries the picnic basket, glancing down suspiciously, after all these years still unable to treat sheep shit and the ground as the same thing. At the north end of the shearing shed we spread a blanket on the ground. Out of the wind we squint up at the brown hilltops. We are resolute about everything—snapping out the picnic blanket, the careful arrangement of cups—for it feels as if we are being scrutinised. Even out here, it is impossible not to think of the strangers.

A faint smell of old death on the edge of the sunny breeze does not escape my uncle's attention. He doesn't like the country. He can't see why we had to drive all this way in order to eat a pizza. There is too much air, too much sky. The line of his jaw turns instantly hard.

Christ only knows whatever made your father think he could be a farmer, he said. He was a perfectly good school-teacher, developing young minds. What was wrong with that? I don't know. Do you, Sport? And, tell me if I'm wrong, but the little conversation he had in him dried up the moment he moved out to the hills.

It was true. My father had grown inward, more silent—in contrast to the noisy arrival of Uncle Warwick and Dawn as they made a big show of trying to step from the car to the house in one easy stride to avoid the sheep shit. But my father didn't regard his silence as a problem, as much as a local condition acquired by anyone who chooses to live in physical isolation.

It takes me a moment to adjust to the surprise, the way you do at a domestic object found in long grass beneath a window-sill, or finding a toy left out in the weather.

After lunch Katie and Ryan run off to explore. Uncle Warwick lies back on his elbows and frowns at an empty paddock. Dawn drops her head and closes her eyes. The sun breaks out from behind a cloud and she pulls a corner of the picnic blanket over her face.

We are an intimate arrangement—my uncle, Dawn, me. But I'm not convinced by it. I don't really belong. And I wonder if that is what Mole had also seen. Some essential difference referred to when he said *You are not like them.*

I lie down on the blanket. As soon as I close my eyes the cage is in my thoughts—I would still be there, half asleep, one eye glued to that unshifting scene in the backyard, but for the banging of a lifting sheet of iron on the shearing shed roof.

I sit up to find the day has changed. Cloud is beginning to

bunch. The wind is getting up, the air is cooler. Dawn is sitting with her knees up, gripping her elbows.

That's when we hear it—a long pealing cry as Katie and the boy come tumbling across the paddock.

It'll be something dead. Trust me, says Dawn.

Uncle Warwick stands up and surveys the acres of grass. I'm telling you, it will be something dead, repeats Dawn.

We find the injured hawk in the far corner of the paddock, its feather-bound fury still intact. Its talons clutch at the air, and its eyes fasten on the sky. It seems to know where the attack will come from.

Uncle Warwick scratches behind his ear, and decides the hawk must have blown against the fence in a gale. But which gale was that? I can't remember a recent storm. A fact that seems to matter less to my uncle than having a plausible explanation.

In any event, Dawn knows how things will go from here. So do I.

She begins to herd up the young ones.

Come on, we are going now. Your father will have to kill it.

My uncle looks surprised to hear this, but he covers up well. He rolls his bottom lip over his teeth and looks hard at the latticed eye of the hawk.

It is left to the boy, all sweetness and light, to ask.

Why?

Because, sweetheart, says Dawn, something else will kill it.

We all nod at the perfect sense of it.

The exact method my uncle will use crosses Dawn's face, a terrible cold knowledge.

She casts her eyes around for the next thing.

It turns out to be the car, and to Katie and the boy, she says, Come on, race to the car. On the count of three.

Dawn sets off at two. Cries of complaint track her across the paddock.

Uncle Warwick makes a move towards the fence and the hawk's eyes roll back.

I have seen it too, the rock my uncle intends to use.

There is a toot from the car, then a longer blast, one of the kids I expect, which causes Warwick to spin around and notice me.

Ah, Sport, he said. Would you mind waiting for me back at the car?

I want to watch. I am used to it.

No, he says. I'd rather no one see.

The side window of the car winds down, and Katie sticks her head out.

What's he going to kill it with?

I hear Dawn say to her, No, Katie darling. That is not something we need to think about.

I bet it's the rock, says the shit-smeller.

Dawn holds up a cautioning finger as I get in the back. Out of the wind, the car is warm with sickly breath. All the way across the paddock I had seen them jamming their hands to their mouths, eating all the sweets.

When we look again, the tall sloped figure of my uncle is dragging his long face across the paddock.

He is quiet when he gets into the car. As he starts the engine, Dawn turns to Katie. Your father cannot kill anything, she says. He even opens windows to let flies out.

I thought it might fly off, said Uncle Warwick. I wanted to give it a chance.

That's all right, says Dawn, and she places her hand over his on the gear stick.

Our farming neighbour, Mr Thorn, had shown me how to stretch the throat of a sheep—you have to grab hold of the snout and pull it back as far as it will go. Mr Thorn stressed the need for a sharp knife and a clear mind. Any hesitation will lead to a botched job.

When we first came to the farm, my father, who had under-estimated this side of farm life, used to get Mr Thorn over to do the killing.

Once he used a sledgehammer to bash Edith over the head. The cow's noises were terrible. They could be heard back at the house, where Mum sat on the floor behind the kitchen door with her hands pressed to the sides of her face. In the end Dad ran across the paddock and fired five rapid shots into Edith. Mr Thorn was astonished that he'd wasted good bullets. It seemed a callous thing to say. But within a year Dad was ready to agree.

A car overtakes us, then another. Uncle Warwick's eyes don't shift from the road. We pass a woman hitchhiker. Only Katie's head turns.

Nobody can stop thinking about the hawk. Except me.

Whenever we returned to the farm from an outing, Dad would stop by the letterbox for me to jump out and open the gate. At the rattle of gate chain, the dogs would start up. The rooster would crow. And, the moment I opened my bedroom door, the budgies would fly against the cage.

~

Toast, he says in that foreign way of his. So that 'toast' is made to sound foreign.

I spread a slice with some leftover chutney.

There is a sticking sound of hurrying feet. Mole butts Doctor out of the way. In an instant his foul morning breath is all over my face.

I would like it with sugar, please. Like I used to have it, he says.

I pass the cup of black coffee through the feeding hole.

20

Colder weather is here—that is my news—and I fear worse is on the way. There is some cloud about. When the sun does squeeze through, it barely makes a difference. To stay warm the strangers have to rush from one side of the cage to the other. They rub their arms. They blow on their hands. Mole jogs on the spot.

There is talk of stocking the cage with hay. Some Trustees resist the idea, they say it is undignified. Not to mention a waste of time. Since the mesh roof does not keep out the rain. Or the leaves. There was some discussion about their collection and disposal. Mr Byrd thought the leaves should be left there as they offer some seasonal colour, especially against the excellent new stonework.

I was pleased to hear my work described in this way, and when I looked up Mr Byrd was ready with a wink.

We could ask the strangers for their opinion, said Mr Wooten. But perhaps not, he said, on second thought. It's probably a moot point. Since the leaves will either disintegrate or blow away.

The terrible silence was ended by Mr Wooten. On a not entirely unrelated matter, he asked. Have the strangers attempted to make artistic sense of their circumstances?

I can point to Doctor's careful separation of the leaves into apricot, yellow, red and brown piles. A bewildering and impressive sight. As colourful as a confectionary shop. Suddenly it was jarring to see the filthy strangers in the company of all that Turkish delight.

What else? asked a tired voice. Mr Bennett has shown signs of stress lately. He complains of broken sleep.

Well, the colder weather has caused some behavioural changes. For example, the strangers stay to the rear of the shitting area, and they are not easily coaxed out.

At the zoo, I often feel the same awkwardness when the Indian rhino labours off to try to hide behind the flimsy tree. Its failure to completely conceal itself doesn't matter. What matters to the rhino is that I can no longer see all of it. It wants or needs some part of its life to remain private.

I have recommended that the strangers' need for privacy be respected for a few hours each day. And, because of wintry conditions on the way, I have also recommended that the strangers receive more food, better food. Carrots produce good nutritional low-cost value. Cereal is even cheaper.

Up to you, Warwick, said Mr Bennett.

Uncle Warwick nodded to show that he had heard.

More worryingly, Doctor has chosen not to eat—a point I left to the very end of the meeting when the Trustees, in their eagerness to get on their way or on to drinks, will quickly agree to an action.

I have tried bananas. Usually he likes bananas. He'll snatch a banana from the feeding hole and carry it to the log. This morning, however, the sight of banana seemed to make Doctor irritable. He had been pacing, hands and fingers interlocked at his back, lost in thought. When I produced the banana I thought he would jog over to the feeding hole. Instead, his eyes narrowed, as if he were annoyed to be dragged away from his thoughts by vulgar appetite.

Mole, who does not care for bananas, sat slumped against the cage wall, his head forward, eyes closed. God knows how he can see through that mop of hair. But he became aware when I reached into the bucket for a carrot. He rolled onto his knees, got up and padded over to the feeding hole for his carrot.

It's nice when we understand each other. It's sad that it so often takes a banana or a carrot—although in Doctor's case, a few bars of Mendelssohn on the clarinet provides him with the same satisfaction.

Mole chewed on the carrot, and Doctor resumed his pacing. When a guest's face covered in shaving cream appeared in an upstairs window, Doctor stopped to pass his fingers across his beard which now has some white in it. He looks so much older than he did when he arrived at the hotel.

But that's another thing. We ought to provide the strangers with proper shaving cream and disposable razors, but when I made the proposal Uncle Warwick glared.

I am more than happy to contribute, I said.

Mr Hughes smiled over his folded arms, as if I were slow. That's not the point, he said, on Warwick's behalf. They could use the razors to harm themselves, he said.

Or someone else, said Uncle Warwick.

What's next? asked Mr Bennett.

Well, like I said earlier, Doctor is off his food, I said.

Is he sick? asked Mr Byrd.

Of course he isn't, said Warwick. He eats as well as anyone in this room.

But, Warwick, the point is he's chosen not to, replied Mr Byrd.

'Enough!' The woeful sound came from the other end of the room. Mr Wooten banged his hands down on the table.

I apologise for the outburst, he said. But, I keep being stopped in the street and asked the same question. Is there any news? I'm sick of hearing the same thing over and over. We need something to show for our efforts.

Oh dear. You would not make a good fisherman, said Mr Fish. I never know what I am going to catch until I have caught it.

Dawn? asked a desperate Mr Bennett. Do you have anything to add?

She looked caught out.

Oh no, she said. No. And she stared into space—which is how I'd found her earlier that afternoon, in the strangers' old room, sitting on Doctor's bed, her hands composed on her lap, her head held very still.

She saw me, and jumped up. She pulled at her dress that didn't need straightening.

I thought I would change their sheets, she said. Could you let the strangers know? And, look, she said. I've put a vase of peonies on their windowsill.

We were used to cleaning the rooms of departed guests, but the strangers had not departed. It still felt like *their* room, and just the other day when Doctor asked, what had become of their room? I was able to tell him, it is still there, waiting for their release.

After the meeting Uncle Warwick asked me to join the Trustees for drinks. It was the first time my uncle had thought to include me. Mr Byrd poured me a beer. As I took the glass from him, he lowered his head near mine. You're doing a fine job, he said. He held his smile. He patted my shoulder and turned to chat to Mr Fish.

Over drinks the Trustees were less testy. Mr Wooten, glass in hand, was jovial, even to the point of being loud. He and his wife had been on a boat trip. A tipsy traveller had fallen overboard. His head burst the surface of the lake, glass in hand. Someone shouted—quick, get a picture. I have it somewhere, he said, and put his drink down to sort through his wallet. And there it was. We grouped around the photo of a man whose mouth was wide with spitting water and joy and, as Mr Wooten had said, there was the cocktail glass held high in the man's raised hand.

For a happy hour or so we forgot about the strangers. And, although only a wall and a pair of drawn curtains separated us from the backyard, the strangers might as well as have been in another country.

I drank quickly. Everyone did. My head was spinning by the time I went down the stairs to my room. I had the feeling I was grinning in the darkness.

And when I lay down on the bed I was helpless to move. And not unhappy about it. There was nothing to do. Nothing to think or worry about. I was airborne again.

21

Lately, doctor has taken to hugging himself and shivering. I understand the request. I put it through the proper channels a week ago.

The blankets should arrive any day now.

When I pass that on, his face remains hinged with doubt.

I would not lie about such a thing. What would I gain from it?

Look, I need your help with something, I say to him.

Mole hears that, and he gets up from the log and comes to join Doctor at the mesh. Help as a word has changed its meaning. Help is now an opportunity to extract something in return.

The map is in my back pocket. I unfold it and spread my arms so it hangs from my fingertips. Doctor's eye scrolls down. Mole stares at a region around my stomach—it could be Central Asia or the Middle East, I cannot quite see. My chin is tucked over the Arctic Circle.

The strangers put their heads together. That, again. One then the other nods.

I know what's coming.

Please. We cannot find it. It is no longer.

We are back in the doldrums, no landfall in sight. This is the hopeless situation I wake to each day. The cage, I've come to realise, is not the problem as much as the stubbornness of the strangers.

It makes no sense at all. Unless, they mean to torture us, to play us like a fish. To provoke us. I refold the map. A stalemate has been arrived at. One lot of conviction set against another.

Now it is their turn to ask. Is there any news? Have you heard anything? They have heard that the woman in the hat has been seen in town.

Their hopefulness is oppressive.

It takes effort to say No as many times as I am required to. Once is never enough to dent the hope radiating back at me from inside the cage.

First thing in the morning it is not so bad. The question is replaced by their appetite. But as they reach the end of their eggs the question returns to their eyes.

When will they be let out?

I would like to be the bearer of good news for a change. At night I dream that the key has been found. I draw back the gate, and the strangers step from the cage with big loony smiles, like beaming astronauts released from a tin can bobbing in the ocean.

You could just release us. Doctor says this so softly that I wonder if I heard correctly.

You could just release us.

Is that what they think? That we are interested in detaining them?

The word *release* catches in Uncle Warwick's throat. He pats his pockets, grimaces. He asks if I have a handkerchief. There is a finger mark on the banister.

Then he notices the metal edge on the carpeted stair that tripped Doctor all those weeks ago. It has lifted again.

The screwdriver is in the office, Sport. Would you mind?

On the desk, he calls after me.

Also on the desk is the photo of Mum and Dad, newly framed. I pick it up, then put it down again. I feel I need to wait for Uncle Warwick to give it back to me.

The Trustees will no longer go down to the backyard to see for themselves. Now, more than ever, so much depends on my ability to transcribe what I see.

They are not interested in what I feel—that is not the job of a witness. They want only to know what the strangers know.

At times it is like watching snails crawl across a path, so slowly does time pass before anything noteworthy happens, and then it might only be that Doctor or Mole had stood and stretched, or that Mole rose from the log and pressed his face to the mesh. These cage movements, as described, fail to tell all of the story. The stretch and yawn do not say enough about their boredom. Mole's face pressed to the mesh does not say enough of his despair. And as the Trustees are interested only in the facts, in this case a stretch and a yawn, they don't get the fuller story of life inside the cage.

The last time I took Katie to the zoo, a passing shower forced us to retreat to the aquarium. Groping around in the fluey breath of the crowd, once more I was struck dumb my lack of ability to describe what I was looking at.

'Yellow' failed to capture this yellow. And the striped thing

I pointed out to Katie was altogether a new kind of stripe—eye-catching, like a zebra I wanted to say, but to call it a 'zebra-like' wasn't right either. Since it fails to capture the rippling line.

Bits of gilded pattern had come apart, bits of seaweed with tiny hands waving on a sinewy current. Lines of colour streamed out of crevices. Orbs of flashing colour as thin as paper glided by. Bodyless heads looked disgruntled, all disapproving eye. Tubular growths with hair lit up as hundreds of tiny bulbs flashed on and off. If I were to encounter any of these creatures in the sea I would have swum away in fright. Yet nothing about them suggested they intended harm. It was a world I had never seen and none of the words at my disposal were of any use in describing it.

But most striking of all was the complete absence of interest by one creature in another.

This evening the cage is bathed in cold moonlight. It looks—well, how should I put this? It actually looks beautiful.

But when I write that down it doesn't seem right. I must have missed something, surely, because it is not possible to think of the cage as beautiful.

I try a new sentence. This time I park the moon a good deal away from the silver-lit cage. And I include the guest in the upstairs window, her elbows resting on the sill, her eyes on the backyard. She gives an impression of thoughtfulness.

Yet the cage is too far away for that thoughtfulness to have any effect.

Doctor is sitting on the log, his elbows on his knees, scratching at the sides of his head. Mole is pissing through the mesh out onto the lawn. Of course he never pisses in the right place. He shits there, but aims his piss our way. At the end of my day's work on the memorial I try not to leave any leftover stones within his range.

Is he aware of the hotel guest in the window above him? Does he care? For all we know public urination is an accepted practice in the place the strangers are from. It is another of those things we are unsure of—and to that growing list I need to add Doctor's smile. After I told him Dawn had changed his and Mole's sheets, he smiled at that news, but his smile seemed also to mock.

Of course I gave a different account to Dawn. I told her Doctor was delighted.

Yes?

Yes, I said. He didn't know what to do with himself, walked in a circle, sat down on the log, stood again. And came back to the mesh, and asked, Would you please thank that kind lady.

And Mole, too?

He said, 'From both of us.'

And Dawn beamed.

22

I have been trying to get on top of a new Mendelssohn piece for Doctor. It's a bit beyond my capability. I start well enough but come to a grinding halt at the same place every time. I should just gallop over those phrases, bluff it out. Sometimes it pays not to look too closely at the notation.

I've just put my clarinet down when there's a pitter patter on the stairs. I know that annoying sound. I wait for her small piping voice.

Have you fed them yet? Mum wants to know.

I don't reply.

And so does Viktor. He said I was to come down and ask you if you are ready, and he said I could feed them if you come with me.

In the kitchen Viktor is preparing the strangers' food. He makes room for Katie at the bench. I need a stool, she says.

Ask nicely, I tell her.

Viktor, can I please have a stool, please?

He gives up the one he is sitting on. He shows her how to cut the carrots and the celery. The celery can be a bit longer, he says. He gets out the cheese and shows her how to cut small sticks that will sit in the clutch of the celery.

Now the knife is in her hand and Viktor is nervous. You won't cut yourself, will you? he says.

A quick shake of her head. She can't speak for concentrating.

Didn't they have this for lunch? I ask Viktor.

He rolls his eyes to indicate upstairs. My uncle is increasingly cost-conscious.

I saw that, the girl says, and the knife flies out of her hand. Viktor, you moron, you nearly made me cut myself.

I pick her up by the shoulders and lift her off the stool. Her feet kick wildly.

Put me down! Put me down!

You don't speak to Viktor, or anyone, like that. Do you understand?

Her mouth is grim. Her eyes are at the point of tears.

Now apologise.

Her chest and shoulders heave.

Sorry, Viktor.

Viktor is delighted, but nervous. He looks up at the clock. It's past feeding time.

On the way we stop for a look from a window. Katie jumps up and down.

I want to see. I want to see.

I pick her up and her face grows still. They're not doing anything, she says. They're just lying in the dirt.

Grass, I correct her. They're lying on the grass.

I want to feed Doctor first, she says.

Why? Are you afraid of Mole?

No, she says.

Are you afraid he will bite you?

She wriggles about in my arms.

Put me down!

Instead I hold her up higher so that now her kicking feet are at the height of the window.

Look, they can see you. They can see your underpants.

Put me down. Put me down. I'll tell Mum.

Ask nicely, I say.

Would you please put me down, please?

Viktor passes her the plate with the chopped carrot and celery and sticks of cheese.

Careful. Hold it with both hands.

If you drop it you will have to eat it, I tell her. The threat is something for her to test her nerve against.

She has to shift the edge of the plate against her hip. Near the cage she selects a piece of carrot. The feeding hole is a bit high for her. She tries standing on her tiptoes, tries to reach the bristled mouth on the other side, and loses control of the plate. She slips and follows the spilled celery and carrot to the ground.

I told you, says Viktor. I told you.

Bits of grass are stuck to the cheese, but she puts it back on the plate, along with the carrot and celery. Viktor has to take the plate across to the garden hose and run the tap to wash each bit of celery and carrot.

I bring over the wheelbarrow and park it in front of the feeding hole. That way she can crouch in it and pass the celery and carrots through.

Mole pushes his mouth wide to the feeding hole.

No! Not him, she says. I don't want to feed him. He pulls faces at me.

Does he? Should we be concerned? It means she has been

out here unsupervised, unless she was teasing him from one of the upstairs windows.

Did you pull a face at him from up there? I ask her.

She won't say.

Well, what do you expect? If you smile, he might smile back, and that way you won't be afraid of him.

I'm not afraid of him, she says.

No, why would you be?

He can't hurt me because he is in the cage.

I'll hold you and you can feed him a piece of carrot to show you are not afraid.

I'm not afraid.

But when I place my hands on her sides I can feel her heart thrashing about inside her ribcage. She holds out a piece of carrot. The stranger has to bring his open mouth closer.

She will need to put her hand through the hole so that the stranger can reach it.

He won't bite me?

Of course not. He's hungry and he wants to be fed. Don't be afraid.

As she reaches into the cage the mouth roars like a lion. The girl reels back, tumbling off the wheelbarrow. She falls awkwardly and grimaces. Her right hand reaches for her left forearm. Then she screams.

An upstairs window opens and Dawn looks down.

Her face disappears, but Viktor is still gazing up at the window. Viktor is older than me, he has more of the world on him, but that counts for nothing in the hotel pecking order.

I tell him not to worry. I'll take care of it. But he can hardly hear me for the bawling of the girl.

And now Doctor shuffles to the edge of the cage.

Please. May I look at her?

Come on, Katie, sit up so Doctor can take a look at your wrist.

Tears are streaming down her white face. The bawling has stopped, but her chest is thumping. Her stretched mouth is held together by a thin line of spittle.

Show me your arm, please, says Doctor.

The French doors to the dining room open. Dawn flies down the steps, then walks as quickly as her tight skirt will allow.

She stops in front of the cage—seeking an explanation—and Doctor looks up. He concentrates on Dawn. He says, Your daughter needs to have her arm X-rayed. I suspect it is a greenstick fracture.

So she will need to go to hospital? asks Dawn.

The girl's top lip shivers and her shoulders begin to quake. Dawn gives her a hug.

There, there, I am sure everything will be all right. At the hospital they will take an X-ray. They'll make it better.

Now she detaches herself. She looks up to attach blame.

How did this happen?

It just did, Dawn. It's nobody's fault. She fell out of the wheelbarrow.

Her eyes shift from mine. She is listening for a false note. She just fell?

Yes. I don't know how else to describe it.

Dawn drops her chin on top of the girl's head. Katie, did you just fall?

Her head nods against her mother.

Mole looks on with renewed interest. So far his roaring has escaped mention.

Now Uncle Warwick appears on the top step. His pasty indoors face winces into the late afternoon sunshine.

What an odd-looking arrangement we are—Viktor, me, Dawn, Katie, tears, consoling sounds, Doctor crouching, nose up to the mesh, Mole staring down at the spilt mess of carrot and celery.

I heard a roar, says Uncle Warwick. He drops down another step and stares.

The girl looks up at her father and sobs.

Warwick raises a hand to his eyes. I thought I heard a roar, he says again.

That evening as Uncle Warwick saunters into the meeting the Trustees flock around him.

Is little Katie all right, Warwick? asks Mr Bennett.

As good as you might expect, he replies.

She's a brave one, that girl. Cheeky, but brave, says the grocer, Mr Hughes.

And Dawn? How is she doing?

Dawn is Dawn, if you know what I mean. She'll be here in a minute.

I don't think there is a worse pain for a parent to endure than the pain of their own child, says Mr Bennett. He pats Uncle Warwick on the shoulder and resumes his place at the head of the long, polished table. He wishes to make a start, but first he repeats his earlier question. And Katie?

Tucked in bed when I last looked.

That's good, says the chair. That's really good to hear.

Then Dawn arrives and everyone stands to offer a new round of sympathy.

She has a cast on her arm, says Dawn. Her cool eye travels around the room. The hospital said it'll be on her for two or three weeks.

That'll slow her down, says Mr Fish.

I'll pass on your well wishes, Eric, says Dawn

Mr Bennett put his glasses on and turned his attention to the agenda I had typed after coming in from carting rocks.

But, before we can start, Uncle Warwick shares what is on his mind. You know, what I find interesting about the whole thing? he says. Doctor volunteered his services.

The Trustees wait. Perhaps there is more.

But what was Katie doing out there with the kitchenhand in the first place? asks Dawn.

It wasn't Viktor's fault, Dawn. I was there too, I say.

She shouldn't have been encouraged. I don't know what you thought you were doing allowing her to feed them. It's undignified.

But the thing is, continues Warwick, Doctor offered to help.

Should I be writing any of this down? I ask the chair.

No, no, says Mr Bennett. We're just clearing our throats. Then he turns to Dawn. Please convey our best wishes to little Katie. Will you do that?

The chair looks down the table to find me.

She received her new tennis balls, did she?

Yes. It's down here on page two of receipts.

Good. Good. That's excellent. Let's start, shall we? Their diet?

Celery and cheese have been added, I report.

No complaints?

No outright complaints, I say.

Perhaps you could advise us about the degrees of complaint, says Mr Bennett.

It's mainly the younger one.

Him again, says Uncle Warwick.

He's not a fan of the celery. He'll eat it but without much enthusiasm.

And cheese?

Yes. I forgot to say. Cheese as well.

What about clothing now that we are moving into colder weather?

You will remember they were given new clothes but they didn't unwrap them. They could not abandon their own clothes without abandoning the lives of those who had worn them. It would complete their erasure. This is what Doctor said. In the end they pushed the new clothes back through the feeding hole.

Yes. I remember, says the chair. Any health matters arising?

Not so far. But there is the matter of sanitation.

For sake of the minutes I would suggest you note 'status quo', says Mr Bennett. Unless anyone feels any differently?

No one does.

23

Where have all the visitors gone? It is three o'clock on a dreary Sunday afternoon. There are some threatening clouds in the west but not enough to prevent the usual crowd from turning up. Except no one does.

Apart from Mr Byrd, who is the only one of the Trustees still willing to be rostered on. He is standing on the porch in his fedora.

The cloud shifted for the steps to emerge from the shadows, and Mr Byrd stepped onto the grass.

But that was half an hour ago. Since then he's fallen under the spell of his own company. He has looked interested in a passing thought. Examined his finger nails. Looked at his watch half a dozen times. There is a temporariness to Mr Byrd, and I am reminded of the strangers when they first came to live in the cage. They too had stood apart from their circumstances—anticipating that things would improve. Their physical person might be restrained, but not their hopefulness, which, in those first days of captivity, had a twitchy bird-like quality.

When so little changes in the backyard, it is hard to keep up interest. Mr Wooten, for example, used to bring a book to read. You see the same thing at the zoo. People dashing by the pens of animals they saw on their last visit.

In Mr Byrd's case, I thought he looked mindful of being on duty, but that duty did not necessarily attach to caring. He jangled change in his pockets. He crossed the grass to poke at the stone rabbit with the toe of his shoe. He spent some time staring at the rusted swing. Then he turned abruptly to look up at the windows, and in my hurry to escape his eye I banged my head. I waited, then looked—I had not been seen. Mr Byrd's face was frozen in thought, like the rabbit's.

It is not a condition that extends to the strangers. Their eyes are like those glassy ones you see in mounted deer. Eyes, but they have no sight. In the case of the strangers, I daresay they could get about the cage just relying on smell.

For some time Mr Byrd showed no interest in the strangers, and nor did they seek him out when, eventually, they ventured into the last patch of sunlight on the floor of the cage. Mole followed Doctor to the mesh.

I left the window, and went downstairs to my room.

The next time I looked, Mr Byrd was over at the feeding hole. He dropped onto his haunches and began to call through the bit of mesh I have still to reinforce with stones. He clicked his tongue, made a coaxing sound. A cigarette was in his hand. It would be like him, even though the general public have been told not to give them cigarettes.

Then he bounced onto his feet, hoisted his trousers, tightened his belt, and moved around to the other side of the cage.

I could tell Mr Byrd found the strangers' silence unnerving, like sitting in a crowded but quiet bus. And, like so many other visitors who similarly find themselves in his situation, Mr Byrd began to whistle.

Later that afternoon a steady *thud thud thud* broke my concentration. I put down my clarinet, and ran outside to find Mr Hughes throwing oranges at the cage. He had a box of them. He was reaching in for an orange, biffing it, then reaching in for another. The strangers, huddled on their log, shuddered as each piece of fruit bounced off the mesh.

Mr Hughes, please, I said, and he allowed me to prise the orange from his hand. He was compliant. It was as though he knew, as a child does, that he'd done wrong.

Look at them, he said. Rubbing their shit in our faces.

You're upset, I said. Would you like me to take the oranges up to the kitchen?

He nodded.

I left Mr Hughes on the porch and gathered up the oranges lying on the ground. A number were bruised or had broken skin. I thought the strangers might like them. Sure enough, they bolted to the feeding hole. I put the rest of the oranges back in the box and returned it to the porch. Mr Hughes was more composed now.

I don't want this coming up in the meeting, he said.

Of course not. You were upset.

I was provoked.

He nodded back at the strangers stuffing bits of orange in their mouths.

Tell Warwick the oranges are on me, my own contribution, he said.

That is generous, I replied.

No. That is what your uncle would expect.

I waited for him to leave before I approached the cage.

The floor of it was littered with orange peel and half-eaten oranges. Juice ran down the beards of the strangers, who tore at the fruit and shoved the flesh into their mouths. The combined smell of orange and shit offered the same smell as garden compost—of things breaking down to create goodness.

The hotel windows report the slow passing of another day. The days are shorter now, the air sharper. In the late afternoon the strangers stand on a fast-shrinking island of light. Their heads turn to follow the sun as it sinks over the rooftops. A lost love comes to mind. A final look homewards as the headland slips beneath the waves. They rub their arms and lift their feet. They are back at a rural railway station, bored, or about to dive into a pool at an unseasonable time of the year. They move closer and closer to one another until the area of light they stand on is no larger than a shoebox. On this last sun-washed island they rub their hands, they rub each other's shoulders. It is one thing to find warmth, it is another to hang onto it. The chewed-up condition of the ground speaks of agitation. New tracks have appeared from another night spent pacing to stay warm. One or two Trustees have wondered if they are mapping out their lost homeland.

The stones do an excellent job of collecting the afternoon warmth. They have definitely made a difference. But for Mole, they are a mixed blessing.

The stone wall on the south side is now waist high. Mole cannot bring himself to look at it. At night we are woken by his screams. Guests complain about the racket, and Viktor is sent out to the backyard to turn on the hose.

In the morning, windows open, faces appear. There is some interest in the cage's inhabitants, but without the galvanising fascination of a few months ago. They are of a more practical concern. Guests are told when it is best to open the windows for fresh air. I cannot take a mop to the shit-stained air. And after all, the strangers have to shit, just as we all do. Those directly above the cage are right in the path of the stench. It rises at night, like swamp mist. Perhaps there is some appeal in being so close to catastrophe. Surprisingly few guests complain.

I was on the upstairs toilet when I heard the shovelling. I finished up, slammed the lid down, and climbed up to push open the louvre window.

Mole was digging with the spade. He worked quickly, throwing dirt behind him. Doctor got up from the log to take over for a bit. His jowls wobbled at the first bit of resistance. He wriggled the spade deeper into the filth and pressed down with his boot. The younger one soon relieved him. And, after that, they took it in turns until they stood in a trench up to their knees. Deep enough to start scratching away at the sides. Deep enough to think that they would soon be able to scramble out.

What to do? I must tell someone. I must tell Uncle Warwick the strangers are digging their way out.

But I also want to see what will happen. It is my job. If I intervene, the Trust may never know. But what do I mean by intervene? What would I do?

In the past, the Trustees talked about the strangers' eventual release. It had always been imagined as a mutually beneficial occasion, peppered with goodwill.

But, here they were—getting away. Well, on their way. And I am torn. I remember how useless the shoebox had looked after my hamsters died. It had been a home. But without the hamsters it was a piece of stinking rubbish that I couldn't wait to get rid of.

As the strangers dig, I feel a surprising allegiance to the cage. Its relevance seems to be on hold. And the catastrophe that we hoped to learn about seems to rest on ground that is shakier than ever.

Then, down in the cage, Mole hits some resistance. As he thrusts with the spade his elbows are thrown back at him. Now he has to chip away with smaller movements. Then he stops, and his head drops a bit. Doctor grabs the spade and begins digging in a new place at the end of the cage. When he thrusts the spade in I hear a metallic ding. The strangers have forgotten. The cage sits on top of an old septic tank.

They lie down on the dirt and spread their limbs. The effort has left them out of breath. For all Mole's press-ups, the cage does not allow for much aerobic activity.

The lights in the rooms are turned off, and the backyard passes into darkness. Out in the street a dog barks. There's a shuffle from the cage. A sniffle. And then, further up the road, the dog barks again, and all joy goes with it as it scampers off into the night.

24

Why don't the flamingos just fly away? asks Katie.

It is a reasonable question. There is no barrier to stop them.

The girl dangles her white plastered arm, and her solemn little face stares at a flamingo lying on the ground in a tangle of neck and feathers.

Some of the birds flap their wings, become airborne just above ground, then drop and bounce along on their long thin legs. Some leap from a standing start.

And then they settle back into creatures of waiting.

Now, home from the zoo, I have a surprise for Doctor and Mole.

In front of the feeding hole I stack towels, and soap, and blankets. And this sends up a tremendous patter of excitement from behind the mesh.

Unfortunately, I am also obliged to pass on some bad news. Bad weather is on its way—wind, rain, bitter cold—and as I announce it the cage suddenly looks more naked and its stone walls sadly incomplete. Perhaps the same thought struck the strangers.

Of course, a weather system like the one expected might blow out to sea. It has in the past. Plenty of times, I add.

But the first piece of news, the fact of the bad weather, is stuck on the faces of the strangers.

Doctor's soft face presses to the mesh. His voice is weak.

The woman in the hat. I believe she was in the hotel earlier.

Where do they get such information?

I don't believe so, but I will check, I tell him.

It would be nice to know before we turn in, he says.

I will find out, and report back. But, look, here are the blankets and the towels.

I shove them through the feeding hole, one at a time, for Mole to pull in the rest of the way.

As each blanket shifts through his hands, he examines it closely, then bites at it with his teeth. He bites and tears until the blankets lie in strips on the floor of the cage.

These he winds around Doctor. His legs first, then his arms which Doctor holds out in front like a shivering child for·his mother to dry.

Then Mole kneels behind Doctor like he is trying to kiss his arse. I wish my uncle could see this. Mole sinks his teeth into the seat of Doctor's trousers. He growls and worries at it, waggles his head from side to side. When at last the trouser material rips, he tears at it with his hands to make the rip longer and better able to accommodate Doctor's toileting needs.

In the early hours I saw Doctor squat. An amazing sight, really, to see a man shit with his trousers still on.

I have assured the Trustees that the daytime temperature is still comfortable for the strangers. By 'comfortable' I suppose I mean adequate.

As far as I can tell Doctor is warm beneath the strips of blanket. The binding may be a practice from their old lives.

The chair takes a moment to digest my report, then glances around the table for Uncle Warwick.

As I understand it, Warwick, the hotel has a plate warmer?

Yes, my uncle says, but the admission turns him gloomy. It won't work without electricity. It is another expense, and one he doesn't mind carrying. What my uncle craves is for it to be acknowledged. A standing ovation would not be out of order. He would be first to wave everyone down into their chairs.

To be used at the hotel's discretion, of course, adds Mr Bennett. I imagine there will be nights when it is not needed at all. But with the weather about to take a turn for the worse—

He broke off to speak to me. You can make a note, I think. Attribute the comment regarding the weather to the Trust as a whole. Of course, we will need an extension cable. Warwick?

Uncle Warwick shifts in his chair. Well if you think it might bring us information, then yes, of course, he says.

Silence. A cough. The rustling noise is Dawn scratching around in her bag.

There is a polite wait. In the end Mr Bennett turns back to me.

And what else?

Well, at night, the strangers walk in a straight line, back and forth. Never in a circle.

Turn, mumbles the younger one.

Turn.

Turn.

All night, until it is no longer necessary to say anything.

Then, at a hideous hour I am woken, the whole hotel is, by

the younger one's screaming. It is up to Doctor to save him from asphyxiation.

Asphyxiation?

Yes. I suspect the stone walls are responsible for him thinking a lid has closed on a coffin that he is inside.

I see. And then?

Then they will trudge in silence, for hour after hour.

Don't they ever get bored? asks Mr Byrd.

I remind him that they have each other.

The stones, Sport, says my uncle. Perhaps you can bring everyone up to date.

The stone wall is now chest high. It has an odd disembodying effect as Doctor greets me first thing. I am thinking of stones, and order. I am always caught unprepared for the long beard and wild hair.

The wall can still go higher. But I may need scaffolding, I say, and the room falls silent.

Well, I think I can arrange that, says the chair, and Uncle Warwick opens his eyes again.

And what about the words for the memorial? asks Mr Fish. Has the muse bitten either of them?

I remind Mr Fish and the other Trustees that the strangers' request for stationery was turned down some time ago.

I think you can put down something to the effect of 'request for stationery to be relitigated at a future meeting', said Mr Bennett.

Pre-dawn, the backyard is still in shadow. Two eyes, bright as stars: a car's headlights sweep the garden wall. And as it progresses up the street, the strangers pick themselves up and

143

begin to trudge from one side of the cage to the other.

I go upstairs to use the toilet off the landing. And, since I'm there, I climb up on the toilet seat for a view of the cage. I see Doctor trip. His knee, I believe. He has been dragging his leg around like a broken wing. Anyway, he trips and sort of splashes onto the ground. After that, he doesn't move, other than to adjust himself a little to see if some extra comfort can be found. A moment later, Mole lies down and curls close behind him.

I had just gone back to sleep when I heard water running from the garden hose.

I pulled back the curtains. Mole stood naked, covered in suds. He swayed, then pushed out his hips and let go a stream of no-hands piss.

Viktor turned off the hose. Mole combed the water off his skin—using the edge of his hand to preserve the dryness of the towel. Doctor, in his rags, squatted over a newly dug hole and evacuated his bowels.

25

The plate warmer is a rectangular metal appliance, about the size of a tea towel, with four short legs. When it was pushed through the feeding hole Doctor received it indifferently. He hadn't been told what it was for, and so passed the gift to Mole, who, encouraged by Mr Bennett, placed it on the ground inside the wall nearest to my basement window, which is where the extension lead will run from.

We had a few trial runs, beginning with Doctor. It is clear how he has aged. He had to sit down in the mud to take off his boot. He needed Mole's help. The moccasin he managed himself.

He showed no discomfort at all as he walked to where the plate warmer sat. Mud stuck to his white ankles, and squelched between his toes.

At such times it is easy to believe we have all been forgotten. The strangers are in their natural habitat, and we might as well be a nearby tree of chattering birds.

It was a pleasant surprise to all when Mole folded up one of the towels and put it on the plate warmer.

Doctor stood by, his face dull. Then, at a signal from Mr Byrd, he stepped onto the plate warmer, and everyone cheered. Doctor nodded, then smiled.

Mr Byrd crouched down on his haunches. Can you feel anything?

Doctor's eyes rose. He waited. He shook his head.

I was about to run off to the room to make sure the power was turned on at the wall, but Uncle Warwick held me back. Give it a minute or two, Sport.

And so, for a few silent minutes, we stared at the plate warmer. We stared at the filthy floor of the cage and at the mud on Doctor's feet. How shiny the plate warmer looked.

Mr Wooten stood over his wristwatch for longer than needed.

Dawn held onto her smile.

All of us were by now trying to stare life into the plate warmer. Inspired by our positive example, Doctor looked down at his feet—until a camera flash caused him to startle with irritation.

Mr Wooten quickly put the camera down. For our records, he explained.

I thought Doctor was about to complain, but then he raised his right foot. Delicately he placed it back down on the plate warmer, and a childlike look of delight spread across his face.

I felt like throwing something up in the air. A streamer or a firecracker. Again, everyone cheered. A few of the Trustees clapped. Mr Byrd smiled broadly, and gave the thumbs up. Mr Wooten's smile was so glassy-eyed I thought he would cry.

Warwick whispered something in Viktor's ear, and the kitchenhand ran off to fetch the bubbly. There weren't enough flutes to go round. I don't like sparkling wine so it was no loss to me to pass my glass through the feeding hole.

Doctor wouldn't leave the plate warmer. Although his

146

interest did dreamily cross to the glass at the feeding hole.

I suppose it was possible to want both things. Doctor wanted warmth, and to have that old world bubbling in his veins. Mole took the flute from me, and held it out to Doctor who surprised everyone by refusing it.

I cannot join in this celebration, he said.

But he showed no sign of getting off the plate warmer.

The chair put a hand on Warwick's shoulder. Now don't go taking it personally, he said. The plate warmer is a good idea. It will improve the lives of the strangers. So what if Doctor lacks the grace to accept a celebratory glass? The whole point about civilised behaviour is that it keeps its own company.

The celebrations drifted to an end, and as everyone filed back inside I slipped away to practise.

After dinner, I was sitting on the bed attaching a new reed when my uncle stuck his head around the door, the extension cord looped in his hand. The cord was plugged into the socket in my wall.

We need to think about when it is appropriate to use this, he said. And, when not to have it on.

He closed the door.

When my uncle said 'we' I had felt the same pleasant feeling of being elevated into the world of decision-making, as earlier in the day, when he said, What do you reckon we put that photo of your mum and dad on the piano?

I could not refuse him.

I picked up the clarinet. I felt a need to play. After a few bars, I stopped. I wanted someone to hear. I needed Doctor. I opened the window and continued. There was an encouraging cough in the dark. I played with full heart after that. I played that clarinet as well as I ever had, and Doctor appeared to me not as he did during daylight, crumbled, a bit broken up and bent at the knee on the plate warmer, but alert and responsive.

I reached the end, and waited.

The night brings everything near. From the cage came a whimpering.

26

Mr Bennett's nightmares start innocuously. A bead of water bobbles, then falls over itself. Now another glistens and runs down the streak left by the previous one. Two beads collapse and chase one another down the widening wet streak. Then a hole in the dam appears, as though punched through by a giant fist. Water bubbles up, then leaps in the air. Another section of the dam dutifully falls away. Section after section crumbles, and enormous sheets of water explode on the river flats far below. The lower bank and hillside are dragged under and the river surges along the valley floor before smashing into a giant concrete rampart and destroying the bridge outside the town. A building leans and falls with calm resignation. Houses topple, a long line of them, like a stack of dominoes.

At which point Mr Bennett wakes—always at the same moment—to tear the drenched sheet off his body. And there is the same confounding day. Mild skies report in through the window. Red geraniums nod in a window box. The irritation of a ringing bicycle bell passes in the street. Yet not a single part of him responds to these things. His heart is still thrashing from an event that never took place.

Now Mr Bennett looks up at the Trustees seated around

him. He is too shaken to notice their startled faces. However hard we might try, it is not possible to feel the nightmares of others. But Mr Bennett's point is understood. The line between what we imagine and what we see is a thin one.

Mole's nightmares are more agonised. Each night he is pulled from a new coffin. His elbows collide with its sides. The upward motion of his head brings contact. He cannot turn over. He is in a concrete culvert and the only thing he can do is keep moving forward, elbows roughed up on the concrete as it slides beneath the drag of his body. It is a long drainpipe he must crawl through—from the sewage pit to where at last he will stand and smell the sweet air of a forest clearing.

But he doesn't always make it. And, night after night, he wakes—screaming—his arms crashing against the wire of the cage and the memorial stones.

Viktor has been told to use the hose sparingly and only as a last resort. In the first instance, he is to go out there and to try to calm things down.

But his shouting makes things worse. In the end the use of the hose seems more vengeful than practical.

I have tried a different approach. I have asked the strangers if they like sports or playing games. Which games did they like best in their old lives?

They regard me as they would a village idiot. Their eyes narrow. Suspicious of where such a conversation might lead.

Who were your favourite sports heroes? I ask.

I have learned not to expect much. Still, it is important to stay the course. And to try to reach out in as many ways as we can think of.

I shave. I wash my hair. I am consistent. But the strangers slide from one day to the next into greater and greater disrepair.

Some of the Trustees wonder if this decline is deliberate, as if the strangers wish to say to the naive visitor, 'Look at us. Look at what we have become through no fault of our own.'

But they have combs, toothbrushes, soap, toilet paper, water, food and blankets.

Tonight is forecast to get down to one or two degrees, cold enough for a light frost. My window is ajar. I wish it wasn't. I can't close it because of the extension cord. Already, the plate warmer has become a nuisance. I could unplug the cord and drop it outside the window. I suppose I could. And that is what I do. I close the window, and dash upstairs to the toilet off the landing. When I push open the louvre window, the feeling is always the same. I am Young Nick clinging to the mast of the *Endeavour*, and there far below is land—and the shaggy head of a strange native who is standing barefoot on a plate warmer.

The native lifts a foot. A pale ankle bone flashes in the light. He is confused. It is not as it was. The world is teasing him.

Mole takes his place. Now they try standing on it together. Doctor with both feet, holding onto the sides of the cage. Mole balanced on one foot and falling away, the other foot trailing in the ship's wake.

I want him to fall in, so to speak, to wave his arms in some madcap plea for mercy above the white caps.

Go on, fall.

Then he does—into the filth, and there he stays, sitting on

his bum, hands propped behind him like it was just a bit of foolish fun.

On the plate warmer, Doctor lifts one foot then the other. Now Mole rolls onto his knees and crawls over. He slaps a hand on the plate warmer, and then they both turn to look across at my basement window. I feel a thrill, a tremendous thrill that only God, on a bad day, must feel when humans make their fatal mistake and plunge over the edge of the ravine.

Meanwhile, the memorial stones continue to mount. They speak of increasing entrapment, of the cage converting to a pen. It looks more permanent, as if built for the ages. Several people have kindly commented that the stones are more pleasing to the eye. And it was Mr Byrd who said the job of the memorial is to provoke our imaginations.

Nobody is saying it has to be real, but to be something we can, and want to, believe in.

This afternoon, Uncle Warwick waited for the shower to pass, then he came out to inspect it. At the sight of the intricately packed stones he began to recollect a Greek holiday he and Dawn had taken years ago, in their youth, scootering around the dry countryside. The air, he said, smelt of wildflowers and stone.

This rare foray into the backyard by my uncle didn't escape the strangers' notice. They pushed their expectant faces into the mesh.

Warwick mistook their interest, and popped inside for some photographs of faded Kodachrome skies, a thinner version of himself astride a motor scooter, beaming with sunburn and temporary Greekness. He held up the photos with his back to the stone wall—and the strangers looked even more haggard behind him. Worn, and in blackened rags, tasselled in Doctor's case. Their faces have lost the ability to hold any expression.

So Uncle Warwick turned to me for a compliment.

Well, what to say? The bandana was a surprise, along with the length of his hair. He could have been anyone other than himself.

With the stone walls rising to new heights there are new shadows for Mole to crawl into. It's easy to forget he is there, but then a ripe smell of excrement will catch in my throat.

Mornings are terrible, but then, when I resumed work after lunch, I almost gagged. Doctor, too. His pained eyes rolled up. With the utmost of dignity he spoke gently through the green mesh. We would like more toilet paper.

We stared at each other, Doctor and I, and the younger one still crouching wet-arsed over a hole.

They have not replied to my sports questions.

I picked up the handles of the wheelbarrow, tipped out a new load of stones, and the dust-choked air briefly obscured Doctor's beggaring face.

I turned to get another load.

He waved away the white dust that filled the air between us.

The other day, he said, where did everyone go?

I couldn't think what he meant.

A week ago, he said. Perhaps longer. It is difficult to keep track of the days. The hotel was quiet. I had the feeling there was no one here.

Oh, that day. Yes. We went for a picnic.

The news appeared to distress him.

You weren't here?

No.

He wriggled his toes deeper into the mud. His lips pursed above his tangled beard.

Who was left to look after us? he asked.

Viktor was here, I said.

The kitchenhand, he said. He looked appalled, as if the command of the cruise ship had been turned over to a waiter.

And an ugliness rose in me. It was a temptation to put the strangers into the same space they have pinned us, and to say nothing. Absolutely nothing, and to stare into space. Then it was as if I had done it, and the instinct was replaced by a feeling of shame. My ears turned red. I wanted to look away from myself.

But there was Doctor. Watchful. He seemed to be assessing someone of unpredictable quality.

I felt we had been left all alone, he said.

We were gone three hours, four max, I said. And don't forget, Viktor was here.

And the toilet paper?

I said I would look into it.

I don't know why I said that. It's not as if I have ever denied the strangers toilet paper or ever would. For some reason in the course of these exchanges I often find myself reaching for the tone of authority. I don't like it. And neither can I explain it. It just rises in me from a place I don't know.

I fetched them toilet paper. Several rolls to make up for the ugliness that had come over me.

In my notes for the Trust there is no provision for me to

report what strange creatures we human beings are. There is no space for me to register these strange new contortions of personality I find myself going through. An admission of that kind would likely alarm the Trustees. They want only to know that everything is under control, that progress is being made.

In one column I write 'three toilet rolls distributed'. I report the day's progress made on the memorial wall. It occurs to me to make a note about the lengthening shadows in the backyard and a wintry hardness that has replaced the autumnal softness that used to include the cage. The air is more sodden, quicker to turn cold. But I'm not sure if this is an observation to pass on to the Trustees. I wonder if it is too much like feelings.

After I'm done with the ledger it is always a relief to turn to the clarinet. A note—any note—cannot be made without feeling. I start with the sheet music, but soon I am improvising. Only one ear is tuned to what I am playing. If I listen too closely I will freeze. I want to stay adrift.

Eventually, I find a phrase to end on. And I wait—one, two, three beats of silence, before there is a smattering of applause. I raise the window further, stick out my head and the hand-clapping grows louder.

What follows is one of those embarrassing moments that I would never jot down in the ledger.

I swing my legs out of the window and cross the lawn to the cage. There is enough light from an upstairs window for us to see one another. The strangers are holding their hands high so I can see them applaud. Mole is not as convincing. But I would expect that. Doctor's shoulders are bobbing and his smiling eyes are flashing at me.

Of course I am delighted.

They must be able to see this, since they carry on with the applause.

Please, thank you, I say, and nod to them both.

Mole drops his hands. But Doctor carries on, just as determined as before.

I make a modest bow. Why not?

Please. That's enough.

As his applause stops the shaggy-haired face surprises with its cultured curiosity. What is the name of that piece?

It is so far from the original, I say, that it would be wrong to give it that name.

Make up any name, replies Doctor. It doesn't matter. It's just for us. That way we will know what is referred to.

'Backyard Pastorale', that's what I will call it.

'Backyard Pastorale', repeats the face behind the mesh.

When I return to my room I plug in the plate warmer.

27

Now that the crowds have thinned, the strangers aren't receiving as many treats as they used to.

Visitors used to pop across the road to the greengrocer's to buy bags of nuts. Mr Hughes kept dozens of small white paper bags tied with a twist on the counter.

Today when I went across to buy avocados for Viktor, the number of unsold white paper bags was embarrassing.

I've fudged the visitor numbers a bit. It's impossible to keep an exact count. I can't be at the window all hours of the day and night. But there are indicators—a certain breathiness in the backyard, the trampled grass. And the bags on Mr Hughes's counter.

Anyway, Mr Hughes gave Katie a bag of nuts to feed the strangers.

She fed Doctor first, a safer option for her to recover her confidence. She began feeding him one nut at a time. Until it occurred to me that this was inappropriate. I said to her that if she were sincere in her wish for the strangers to have the nuts then she must hand over the bag for them to help themselves. It is more dignified.

Doctor, however, didn't seem to care. He wanted a nut more

than anything else in the world and didn't care how it arrived. His unshaven mouth opened. Katie popped the nut in, then jumped up and down squealing with naughty delight. I had an idea he must have nibbled her finger. I grabbed the bag of nuts off her and threw it through the feeding hole. The strangers flailed after it.

The girl yelled at me, I wanted to feed them! You said I could.

You can, but not by hand. You have to pass things through in the proper fashion.

We watched the strangers for a while. Listened to the rustle of paper and their grunts. Sometimes a single nut got lost in the folds of their palms. They had to lick it up out of their hands.

Katie grew restless.

I saw Viktor chuck their food, she said, and it landed on the ground and got all yucky.

Well, Viktor shouldn't do that. It is not nice. You must tell me if you see him do that again.

He did it yesterday. I saw him. You weren't there. He threw a baked potato and it landed on the ground.

I couldn't recall seeing a baked potato inside the cage.

That's because they ate it, said the girl.

The strangers were still working their way through the bag of nuts when Uncle Warwick appeared on the porch in his tennis whites, with a white towel around his neck. He held up my racquet. I had forgotten it was a tennis evening.

A starry night, another heavy dew is on its way. The strangers are asleep in the dirt. Doctor on his favoured side. All the grass inside the cage has disappeared. Were they sheep they would be looking withered by now. Their ribs would show.

They have made their world small. As a result, they are tired, and bored.

What more can we do for them? ask the Trustees.

I suggested that we encourage them to grow their own vegetables.

Mr Hughes raised an eyebrow. He needn't have worried. The strangers' dietary needs barely make a difference to the hotel's weekly order from his store.

What kind of vegetables? Tomatoes? Courgettes? Butter beans? It is surprising how out of whack townspeople are with the seasons.

I recommended potatoes and silverbeet. They will be ready in late winter.

Late winter? That produced some nervous noises around the table.

Not cauliflowers? asked Mr Wooten.

Mr Hughes snorted, and left it to me to pass on to Mr Wooten that cauliflower is an autumn crop.

Uncle Warwick was surprisingly receptive to the idea. We went out and bought some seedlings. I wasn't sure if the potatoes would be ready in time, so I added carrots.

At first, the strangers were surprised, even excited. But when they learned the date for harvesting, Mole howled and punched the mesh. Doctor began to hyperventilate. From the other side of the stone wall I encouraged him across to the log, and there he sat, with his head in his hands.

I felt a bit foolish holding the trays of little plants with their innocent little green heads.

So I left them on the ground beneath the feeding hole. I thought I would give them time to get used to the idea.

The other day at the zoo Katie and I had watched ducklings paddle on the pond. They seemed to be flagbearers for everything that was good in the world.

An hour later, the tiny green plants nodding in the breeze similarly affected the strangers.

We discussed where to plant them. I wondered if a patch could be measured out between their shitting area and the log. In time, a small green screen might provide some privacy. But Mole was reluctant to give up any of their recreational space.

Doctor hadn't shifted from the log. Now he pointed to the ground in front of him. I saw what he had in mind. A small garden for himself to sit in.

I passed the trays of seedlings through the feeding hole. A tremendously civilising transaction, as I experienced it. But later I could not find a way to say as much in the ledger. To recall the mutual smiles and nods of appreciation made no sense. In the end I settled for 'A successful planting, three rows: silverbeet, carrots, potatoes'. The strangers dropped to their knees, Doctor with the spade and Mole using his hands, to dig three furrows in the dirt. There was no need to explain anything. Mole appeared to know the ideal planting distance between each silverbeet.

If they are still there in the spring they can try their hand at growing tomatoes.

28

Ever since the plate warmer was introduced Doctor has not worn his footwear. The moccasin and laceless boot sit tidily together at one end of the log. The Trustees are astonished, and I have told them that, to be honest, I can't imagine him ever putting them back on. His feet are so filthy. They are caked with mud. I might believe it was intentional, a clever way of sealing in warmth. But a new dullness in his eyes suggests otherwise.

It's been a surprise to everyone to see Doctor let himself go. He lives only for the plate warmer. I switch it on, and a greedy relief floods his face—he is like a man sinking into a warm bath.

The clean state of the log has become a point of domestic pride. For Mole, especially. He will spit on it and rub away with a towel. As a result, it is shiny, like a length of scrimshaw. I was tempted to give him a nail or a screwdriver just to see what carving might produce.

Doctor is happier in the dirt. He's like an old croc sliding between the swamp and the bank.

Years ago, on a holiday snorkelling trip, I had floated along on the lid of the sea, gazing down at all manner of colourful things scattered below me. I had felt both part of and separate from the water.

I don't feel the same way when I look from the window down at the strangers. I don't feel that we share the same world at all. The stone walls of their pen belong to another place. It is in the backyard, but it does not belong to the backyard.

The backyard has been closed to the public for a week now. Out of sight, but not out of mind.

Everyone in town knows about the closure. The topic hovers in the air, unspoken, in the greengrocer's shop. The customers concentrate on the trays of apples and pears. But I know I have been seen, and that my presence forces unpleasant thoughts on them. I wonder if they wish I wasn't there at all.

This morning the dew on the grass has a hard glint to it. It's as if it means to hurt and knows it has only a limited time to do so. I have on a woollen beanie, a scarf and Dad's mustard-coloured corduroy jacket.

Dad used to wear the jacket all the time. He was an odd sight at first. Out in the weather, wading through paddocks of sheep. He looked like a man from the city, especially in Mr Thorn's company. Mr Thorn wore the appropriate wet-weather gear, a hood and waterproof pants. But there, striding along-side, was my father in a corduroy jacket.

Today is the first time I've worn it in the backyard. Mole pushed his face into the mesh and stared like a small boy who has seen something he wants in a shop window. I suppose the colour caught his eye. The warmth of it. The collar has a woollen lining.

If I thought he would wear it, I would give it to him, I

think. But the idea of pushing it through the feeding hole for him to touch with his grubby hands only to decide he cannot wear it made me reluctant. Also, I am squeamish. I've never been one to eat off another's plate. I can't share an ice cream. I wouldn't want the coat back. Bearing in mind, it has been some time since they requested the hose.

Still, he couldn't stop looking at Dad's corduroy jacket.

The floor of the cage moved, and Doctor got up in that broken-bodied way of his, his feet sliding in the mud—a pair of watery eyes lift above his matted beard.

You didn't turn it on, he says. All night. Nothing.

No.

I fill their cups from the tea flask. Doctor takes his from the feeding hole. His fingernails are black. The strangers have requested nail files. I make a note to remind Dawn.

I have some news. But first I wait until Mole has placed a towel on the log and they are both sitting down. There are new rules. Between 8am and 10am and 8pm and 10pm the plate warmer will be switched on.

Mole's arms stay folded. His eyes haven't shifted from my corduroy jacket. Doctor's hands are set on his thighs. His head is lowered towards the vegetable patch.

Tea. Toast. Three slices each (officially). Still no raspberry jam for Doctor.

I watch them eat. I wait until there is some warmth inside them, as there is more bad news.

The forecast storm, I remind them, did veer out to sea. We clipped its edge. Cooler air, a shower or two at night. You might recall.

They stare back at me. They wait.

Unfortunately, a new storm is coming.

Then you need to get us out, says Doctor. His weak eyes dare me to disagree.

Well, yes, of course, I reply. That would be the perfect solution. But you know the problem. It has been explained.

Doctor's eyes scope the backyard.

It has been some time since we've had a visitor, he says.

The backyard is closed, I tell him, until the memorial is finished.

He looks alarmed.

Closed? Why didn't someone say? We should have been notified.

Well that's what I am doing now, I reply.

Yes, but it just came up in conversation. I would have thought we would be told officially.

He looks nervous, jittery. He doesn't know what to do with his hands. I had hoped, he says, we might hear 'Backyard Pastorale' again.

I wait, and let the silence do its thing.

It has been so cold, he says. What will become of us if we are not let out before winter?

Mole sticks up his hand. I wish to say something, he announces.

Yes.

A flock of geese.

Geese?

Big brutish geese. Bigger than an aeroplane, horrible things, silver bellies breathing fire out their eyes.

I reach into my back pocket for my notebook.

'Geese.' I write that down.

No, no, says Doctor. He was joking. You were joking, weren't you, he says to Mole.

The smiling Mole won't say or meet his eye.

I write that down too. 'Geese. Joking.'

Doctor shakes his head. No, no, he cries. We are being punished. Punished beyond any reasonable measure.

His eyes drop to the pen and notebook in my hand. It is impossible for a face to keep all its figuring out on the inside.

All right. Look, he says. I don't think there was any smoke. But if there was, I can't tell you why. You see, I am not even sure of that detail.

All the same I write down 'Smoke'. It is something, even if it is a lie. A lie is something. Why should the strangers' mendacity be ruled out? Or their imaginary lives?

I finish making my note. Is there more? I don't want Doctor to think that he has in any way paid for extra time on the plate warmer. I put on my unimpressed face, the same blank expression that meets my eye whenever I glance up from discharging my report to the Trustees.

He says he can tell me about the road and their journey here to the hotel, and their lack of appetite.

But this is something he has said before. The lack of appetite. The aimlessness of their flight. The lost horizon back over their shoulder.

Back in my room I pull out the extension cord. It's time for my own breakfast. Viktor has promised fresh croissants.

On the landing I run into Uncle Warwick. He has one hand on the banister and is bending down to rub his calf.

I felt something go, he says. I ran wide for that forehand and I felt something go.

I don't remember my uncle running wide for anything. But, as he has an injury an event must be created to explain it.

So, what's going on out there, Sport?

They were attacked by giant geese, I tell him.

Uncle Warwick is interested.

Fire-breathing geese larger than aeroplanes, I say, and his mouth buttons up. His face grows cold.

Who said that?

The younger one.

I really dislike him. I'll tell you something else. Dawn can't stand him either. He flashed his genitals at her, did I say?

No. Are you sure?

My uncle doesn't answer. I suspect Doctor happened to be hosing him down, and Dawn happened to wander into the line of sight.

He's not on the plate warmer, is he? says Uncle Warwick

We move to the window. Down in the pen Doctor is on the plate warmer. He is looking down at his disgusting feet. It is also clear that he is talking to himself. He steps off the plate warmer. Back in the filth, he walks in a little circle as if hoping for better news on his return.

Their world looks so small. It has just one sun in it, and that is the plate warmer.

They'll soon figure it out, says Warwick.

Rain this evening. Well, a passing shower. Still, the Trustees were glad to get in out of it.

We moved through the agenda with unusual speed, hastened by the odd flash of lightning in the window and the hammering effect of the rain on the roof. Muffled assents, throat clearances, nods here and there. Later, downstairs, I struggled to put a face to any of the half-said things.

When the rain stopped, they breathed more easily, and fired questions at me as they came to mind.

The strangers' recreation area?

That news is far from pleasant. As their shitting area continues to grow, their recreational area decreases. It's just one of those things.

What about the woman in the hat? asked Dawn. Do they still ask after her?

Oh, yes. They talk about her at night. A week ago, Doctor was certain she was in the hotel.

Who might that woman be? pondered Dawn.

The question found no takers. The Trustees moved down the agenda without her.

And the plate warmer? asked Mr Byrd. Is it at last bearing fruit?

I wish I could say, yes. I don't want the Trustees to feel discouraged. If the plate warmer was a woman, I would be inclined to tell them that Doctor had fallen in love. When it's turned off you would think there is nothing else for him to live for. He lies in the dirt, waiting for daybreak. I switch it on and his whole body pants.

And what about transgressions? That old question. It's as if the Trustees want to feel enraged and that it is up to me to feed that flame.

I open my ledger and flick through the pages.

Yes. Two days ago, there was an incident.

Viktor was spooning egg into Doctor's mouth when for no good reason Mole urinated through the cage onto Viktor's foot. I think he got his leg as well. Viktor leapt like he had been bitten and threw the spoon over the garden wall.

The Trustees were appalled. They were also thrilled.

But why would he do a thing like that? The world is a filthy place for a man like Mr Wooten to live in.

I can't think why, I said. The eggs were cooked just as the strangers like them. Not too runny. Not too hard.

God help me, cried Mr Wooten. What would possess a man to urinate on another?

The question went unanswered as Viktor, fresh from feeding out, arrived with the drinks trolley. He dragged his leg across the room, the urinated-on one, as if he had been wounded by gunshot.

Is that it, Sport? My uncle was eager to move on to drinks.

There was more to report. But I wondered if it would be wise to share, since it involves my own shortcomings and reliability. They know I can't be at the window all hours of the day and night. But, just as importantly, even when I am I can't be depended on to see everything.

For example, this afternoon, Viktor left a plate of cake on the grass beneath the feeding hole. I would not have noticed it but for the strangers pushing their faces against the mesh. They tried to see over the tips of their noses. The cake looked abandoned. Or stolen. One of those situations where the bandits successfully rob the bank but in their getaway drop the bag of money. Viktor must have been called inside, then forgotten about the cake. I could have gone out there and fed the cake to the strangers. But I needed to see the event play out on its own. Then, as it happened, Katie showed up—unaccompanied. And that changed things. I thought I had better go out. Mole doesn't like her. She knows that. She made sure she had his eye, then she trod on the cake.

Then Dawn ran out. She saw the ruined cake and put it down to Katie's clumsiness. Still, I was pleased to hear her blame the girl. So was Mole. Dawn said she would get Viktor to bring out two new slices of cake.

No, said Mole. I want that one.

And he pointed at the cake Katie had stepped on, and he smiled at her until I thought Katie might burst into tears.

Then, for no reason that I could see, the girl's face lit up. She started jumping up and down with excitement. My confusion lasted a few more seconds. Often what I see out the window is shaped by some event that I cannot see. In this instance, the arrival of Katie's friend, Ryan, the shit-smeller.

The two of them set off running around the cage making whooping noises.

Doctor sat in the mud, his hands slapped against his ears, until at last Dawn led the noisy racket inside with the promise of a treat.

Mole went on raking his bare foot back and forth in the dirt. Then he crossed to the other side and he marked out another destination point. Back and forth he went, twelve paces in each direction—as if he were setting out on an expedition. Doctor got to his feet and joined in.

It amazes everyone how much they are able to get out of that small space.

29

A few spots of rain land in the stone dust. I pick up the handles of the wheelbarrow and by the time I reach the backyard the rain is sweeping in. Grey lines of it that have driven the strangers back against the cage wall, and there they huddle, Mole on his haunches, staring out at the world with dead eyes. Doctor gamely on his feet, but bent forward, a hand on each knee.

I abandon the wheelbarrow, and run inside. My shirt is wet through. In the ledger I scribble down a brief note about the wetness of the rain. An hour later the strangers are grey blurry figures. They have given up trying to shelter and have chosen to pace. As they make their way from one side of the cage to the other, they struggle to stay on their feet. Mole has to grip Doctor by the arm.

Each time they arrive at the side of the cage closest to my window the strangers look up. They are stunned. Their faces are plastered. They have lost their way. Then one or the other remembers: they must keep moving.

Doctor lifts a sodden foot and as it lands in the mud Mole turns him, gives a light shove at the shoulder, and off they go. They trudge with no end in sight. Doctor's misery stops at the end of his nose. He is in his own world. And I am in mine.

What to do? I pick up the clarinet. But the rain is too loud. If the strangers were to yell out, no one would hear them.

In any case, while I am prevaricating the rain passes over and the two soaked figures come to a halt. Wet shirt sleeves hang from their wrists. They look up at the sky.

Water is running from wherever it has collected. It gurgles in the guttering.

In the washed air the strangers' voices sound nearer. Walk, commands the younger one. Doctor nods, but as Mole's hand lands on his shoulder he breaks away. His eyes glisten behind his beard as he steps onto the plate warmer.

I let the curtain go. All the way up to the first-floor landing I can hear him shouting at the windows. I drop the toilet lid and climb up. I stick my head out.

Doctor is still on the plate warmer—he won't budge—and his head is turned to Mole who is trying to reason with him.

I think about turning the plate warmer on. It is outside the permitted hours, but given the conditions…On the other hand, what if it rains again, what if the plate warmer develops an electrical problem, blows a fuse? It is one of those things that I need to explain to Doctor—he is still shouting and waving his fist at the world.

We must walk, Mole tells him. We have to walk.

Doctor looks down at his feet just in case the plate warmer has magically transformed itself into a warm bath. No? He closes his eyes and steps back down into the mud and sets off after Mole. *Slop, slop, slop.*

The rain returned that night—it pounded the backyard. It was like the sound of crashing waves. It was hard to hear properly but I could have sworn Doctor yelled 'Paris!'

Rain spilled off their bright noses. The stench of shit rose to the window—lit pools dancing in the rain. A lake formed inside the cage and spread onto the lawn.

I pushed the window wider.

Slop, slop, slop.

No! cried Mole.

Doctor's reply sounded almost gleeful. Yes. Yes. I told her. A long miserable line of us stuffed with the same unsatisfactory French breakfast.

These utterances of Doctor's came in a wayward rush, like a spring tide intent on claiming for itself what normally lies out of bounds.

Turn! shouted the younger one, and the conversation drifted away from me, replaced by the steady fall of rain.

The strangers paced, with their wet glowing faces. Rain bounced around their feet.

I closed the curtain and got ready for bed.

It was still dark when I woke. But I got out of bed and pulled back the curtain.

Under a spreading grey sky the cage was visible. The stones looked quite wonderful at this hour, like they had been there for centuries.

Two sodden shadows leaned one against the other. I wasn't surprised when Doctor slid off the shoulder of Mole and dropped face-down into the mud.

Mole bent down, and his head disappeared from view. Then he rose, and Doctor after him, held up like an article of clothing pegged out to dry.

Mole put a hand to his neck to correct a crick. From holding Doctor up, I imagine.

Off they set, sliding and listing, like a couple of drunken fools.

Turn!

Turn! repeated Mole, and this time Doctor obeyed—slipping and sliding—before Mole caught him. I thought Doctor looked smaller, reduced somehow, by the rain.

I shut the window, closed the curtain and sat down at the desk. What to write? What do the Trustees need to know? They are desperate for some sign of progress. There has been no catastrophe visited upon us, nor any signal that one is on its way.

In the ledger I write 'rain', enter the date and add 'a restless night'.

A pink glow in the sky. Shining grass outside the cage. Nodding blue flowers. It was very pretty. Everything dripping. The mesh. The garden wall. The gutters. Out on the road, stormwater drains gurgled and burped.

Doctor lay in a puddle. The younger one sat in the mud, his back against the mesh and stone.

The rain returned, heavier and heavier until the strangers disappeared from view.

In the kitchen I ate my sausages and eggs. Viktor complained he'd hardly got a wink of sleep for the rain. Uncle Warwick came in looking morose. Tennis had been cancelled. Then the phone down in the lobby rang and he hurried off. Dawn came in to make herself a slice of toast. She looked across to the window, shoved a corner of the toast in her mouth, and went on staring at the window.

Was it bad down there last night? she asked.

'Bad' is one of those words that the Trustees find unhelpful. Who is to say what is or isn't bad?

It was dark, I replied. Conditions made it difficult to see.

She looked at her toast without much appetite, took a bite and then looked at me. Sometimes I get into a staring contest with Mole. But with Dawn it was different. I wanted to screech at her like a baboon. The contest had hardly started when she turned away. She looked frightened. It was as if everything private in her had been thrown open for others to see. It didn't last long. Her face hardened and she shoved the toast back in her mouth.

I finished the last sausage, carried my plate to the dishwasher and went downstairs. As soon as I opened the window, the skies caved in. In an instant the cage disappeared from view. Obviously, it was too wet for the plate warmer. I closed the window. What now? Clarinet? I picked it up, listened out to the weather, then put it down. The rain had stopped. Just like that. It could not make up its mind.

A patch of blue sky appeared. I stuck my head out.

The stone walls shone. There was no sign of the strangers. For a second I thought they had escaped and I felt a giddy, almost sick excitement rise in me. This is what the backyard would look like with the strangers gone. A crude piece of tea strainer sitting inside four lines of dry-packed stones. Denied of its practicality the cage looked like a folly.

I ran to the window upstairs, stood on the toilet seat and looked out. And there they were. A creature stirred in the mud. It rolled onto its hands and knees.

Viktor knocked the top off a boiled egg. Doctor crawled to

174

meet the teaspoon of runny egg with a grateful mouth. He kept his mouth open. The egg was hot.

And I made you some fresh tea, Viktor announced.

Hot tea. The marvel of it drew old courtesies out of Doctor. Would you care for a sip from my cup? the mud-soaked creature asked Viktor.

No, thank you, replied Viktor. I have my own. Besides, I can make myself a cup of tea whenever I like.

Doctor stared at the kitchenhand—at the wonder of it.

Viktor so enjoyed seeing the effect of his words that he repeated them to the Trustees later that evening when he wheeled in the drinks trolley.

The older one was lying in shit, he began. I went over with the eggs and told him I could make tea any time I liked.

The room fell silent. Uncle Warwick got up to show Viktor to the door. On his way out, Viktor kept looking back, apparently confused.

Uncle Warwick closed the door and sat down again.

I opened the ledger and read. 'Rain.' 'A restless night.'

Mr Byrd interrupted. I would have thought the rain would have done the trick. I mean, if they are withholding anything, surely to God last night was the time to wave a white flag and cough it up.

Mr Wooten shook his head. Their defiance is remarkable, he said.

The comments angered Mr Bennett. It was a deluge all over the district, he said. There are land slips outside of town. Stock losses.

Several faces turned to the window. A chair leg scraped the floor, but no one rose.

The backyard seemed as far away as ever. It was like hearing that a ferry had capsized with a colossal loss of life. A tragedy, yes, that everyone could agree on without actually feeling anything.

There was talk of getting some plastic sheets from the garden centre to drape over the mesh roof of the cage. But it seemed a little late for that. A bit like throwing a life jacket to a floating corpse.

Mr Wooten thought of getting in an excavator and digging them out. Mr Bennett waited until the excitement had died down, and then he reminded the meeting of the sewage pit the cage was built over. Concrete. Reinforced concrete. Impossible.

It was upsetting. The whole night had been. What with the rain. The waiting. The misery of not knowing. And the anticipated storm that was still to arrive.

The meeting was called to a close. No one felt like staying on for drinks. Everyone wanted to get home before the next big front arrived.

30

There was a flash and the backyard filled with brilliant colour. The mesh shone with a kind of television brightness and the wet clothes of the strangers turned black.

Doctor tried to engage me.

I dreamt last night there was some news, said the dishevelled creature from behind the stone wall.

I put down the rock I was holding.

It turned out to be a mistake, he continued. Not the dream. But, in the dream, the mistake was acknowledged and we were allowed to go on our way.

I know it is important to keep up their spirits. And I do try. Earlier, I passed a small amount of straw through for them to pack around the silverbeet shoots in their little garden.

At first Doctor looked confused. Then he changed his tune. Thank you, he said. We are extremely grateful. But is there any news?

Your situation was discussed by the Trustees last night, I replied.

He turned to Mole sitting on the log. Did you hear that?

Mole did not reply, but continued to stare at the vegetable patch.

I then had to explain that I am not allowed to divulge what is discussed by the Trustees. It would be a breach of confidentiality.

You understand?

Yes, replied Doctor. But I wondered if…perhaps…if there was some news. Concerning us directly.

When I didn't reply, his mouth dropped. The dream, it was so real, he said.

I had a strange urge to reassure him, as we do a child whose belief in Father Christmas has just been shattered.

He left me and stepped onto the plate warmer, and waited with the kind of resignation seen on the faces of people standing at the bus stop.

I wheeled the empty barrow away. At the front of the hotel I ran inside to turn on the plate warmer even though it was outside of permitted hours. Then I refilled the barrow and pushed it around to the backyard again.

Mole looked a bit distracted as he urinated. Just his upper body showed above the top line of stones.

Doctor now sat on the plate warmer. He was warming his bum, blowing on his hands. Shoving his feet into the dirt like he was pedalling a bike. Around his naked feet the mud went on making a popping sound.

I got into a good rhythm packing stones and soon forgot about the strangers, even Doctor, sitting on the plate warmer, mumbling his nonsense about the woman from the agency. The woman in the hat. A legendary figure able to scale walls, walk through fire, and step across oceans.

I slapped down another layer of stones, and looked up at the first spit of rain.

All day the weather couldn't make up its mind. Still one moment, gusty the next. A blast of cold air passed through the backyard and I had to dash inside for the corduroy jacket. Mole's quick eyes noted it, then both strangers looked anxiously up at a large patch of blue sky being slowly erased by a dark front.

They ducked before I felt it—a tremendous gust of wind that slapped us. Then everything was still again. Now a second slap. This one was more forceful. It pressed against the side of the hotel and held us there as more wind came whistling out of the hills. Leaves and twigs flew against the windows. Another gust thumped the hotel. I heard later that a number of bar regulars rushed into the lobby to look up at the swinging chandelier.

In the backyard the wind was more confused. The strangers had their arms spread against the mesh. The younger one stood firm and resolute, his eyes closed. The rag-tasselled Doctor shook and trembled.

A day later, everyone had a story to tell. A split tree glared from a hilltop. No one had ever seen such nakedness. The hills were still bruised. During the worst of the gale sheep had lain low in the grass, converting an entire paddock into white stepping stones. After a concrete water trough was blown over, cattle stood around looking at the ground. It was unnatural for wind to push rocks around like kernels of corn, but no one could think of another explanation for the large boulder that had shifted to the middle of the road leading out of town.

Then the madness stopped—all that screaming in the tree-tops and under the eaves. It stopped and the air turned into listening air.

We gathered at the upstairs windows. Few of the Trustees showed any interest in the cage below. Everyone's attention was on the menacing dark cloud inching in from the south. And as the windows looked out on our behalf, the same windows seemed to look in on us as though they were the eyes of the coming storm.

The rain returned in the early evening, soft, with a few fat showy drops. An hour later the strangers stood in a downpour, unable to move.

In one extraordinary burst every tap in the sky was turned on, and the stinking mud from the cage washed across the backyard lawn. The rain drowned out every other sound in the world. I stayed at the window and watched the strangers dissolve inside a wash of water and white air.

Then the downpour ended—stormwater drains bubbled and frothed and brown lakes spread across roads and lapped at doorways. A hole in the sky appeared—pale at first, then blue, starkly blue, like the bluest of heart-stopping blues.

I was about to go outside and check on the strangers when a number of raised voices surged through the hotel. The dining room door burst open and the tail end of a heated discussion streamed out to the sodden world of the backyard. Viktor, Uncle Warwick and Mr Bennett on the tail of Bill Francis's leading farmhand, Joe Phillips.

They stormed up to the stone walls of the memorial. The strangers must have been sitting or crouching because the party had to stand on their toes to look over the walls. It was like a scene from the stockyards. Men each with a foot up on a railing. They looked over the stock with seasoned eyes. Viktor was the odd one out. He didn't count. Of course, he didn't know that.

All right, I heard Uncle Warwick say. Take the younger one. He won't go far without Doctor.

Understood, replied the farmhand.

Now Mr Bennett turned to my uncle. Ball's in your court, Warwick, he said.

My uncle glanced around. He looked across at my window. But at hearing the feet stomping in from the country I had raced up to the toilet off the landing for a better view.

Warwick, said Mr Bennett, once more.

By now the strangers' faces were up at the mesh. I could hear the younger one ask, Has she come? Is she here at last?

Warwick's hand made a jangling motion in his pocket. His other hand passed across his chin, and he produced the key.

The strangers rushed to the gate.

Uncle Warwick turned the key in the lock. The gate swung back, and Mole flew at him. Uncle Warwick's head snapped back. The stranger went to throw another punch but found his arms tangled up in the farmhand's. Mole sagged immediately. It was as though that one punch had exhausted him. Joe Phillips went on bear-hugging him. The stranger kicked his feet a bit but the struggle had gone out of him.

Viktor yelled, I told you! I knew we'd need a sack!

Warwick waved him silent. His eyes lifted nervously to the guestroom windows. That is when he might have seen me, but he didn't. He put a hand to his mouth, then looked at it for traces of blood. His face was white, but when he spoke he sounded calm, as if it were a dream he was recounting.

I'm fine, Viktor. Really. Thank you. And when you stop to think about it…well, it's perfectly understandable after all the rain we've had…

181

Mr Bennett nodded back at Uncle Warwick. He was almost convinced. He most sincerely wanted to be.

They're animals, said Viktor.

No, said Uncle Warwick, as calmly as before. We don't know who or what they are, and that is as much our problem as theirs.

His restraint was remarkable. He sounded so composed that I began to wonder if the blow to his head had caused a personality change.

Now Joe Phillips spoke to Mole. I'm not interested in any fun and games. You understand?

Mole didn't reply. He looked like a carcass hanging off a hook in a kill shed. His feet were still off the ground. Joe stood him up properly. We have a real crisis on our hands. Five hundred or more at risk, he said.

At hearing that figure Mole's face reddened. I thought he looked ashamed.

As Joe spoke, he concentrated on the chair. I couldn't hear what he said, partly because Uncle Warwick shifted himself into the conversation and the words became walled up by coats and hats. But I did hear Joe Phillips say, You can sort all that out later.

His hand was still clamped onto Mole's shoulder.

What about the other one? asked Mr Bennett.

There was Doctor wrapped in his sodden shitty rags peering out the open gate of the cage. His feet seemed to anchor him— he could go no further. He leaned forward, peered, then reached to push at the air in the opening. There was something he wished to say. Something on the tip of his tongue.

Joe Phillips got in ahead of him, and addressed his remark

to Uncle Warwick. I don't want to sound harsh, but I don't think he's much use to us, he said.

The gate swung shut. Warwick put the key in the lock and turned it. The group of men walked up the path and disappeared inside the hotel.

Alone, under the dripping meshed sky, what Doctor had wished to say now bubbled out of him.

I would like something to eat, he said. And, I would like a bath.

He cocked his ear. He waited for the world to hear.

No one heard. No one other than me.

I was stunned. What would I enter in the ledger? What to say about the ease with which my uncle had produced the key? I had seen something I couldn't unsee.

The story had just taken a big leap from the official account and, as far as I could tell, without explanation or remorse.

Might there be an explanation? Might the key have turned up? Perhaps there had only been time to phone Bill Francis and Mr Bennett, and then everything had happened as I saw it.

It was possible.

Still, a new explanation would be needed to take the place of *the lost key*, and I suspected that would be my job. And, it also occurred to me that this new account might come down to what I might admit having seen and what I might choose to leave out.

I got down off the toilet. I wished to God I hadn't seen any of it.

31

For Mole the trip through the hotel to the waiting truck was a journey into an old and familiar world—the soft tread of the carpet, the warm domesticated air, a mingling of aerosol, hairspray, deodorants, floor cleaner, wood-panelled security— then out to the watery drive and a gloating sky.

A number of men I didn't know were crammed in the front of the parked farm truck. They looked up with interest as the stranger emerged from the hotel. The sight of him seemed to exceed everything they had heard.

Mole appeared uncertain. He blinked at all the new available space and seemed astonished by it.

Very slowly he set off across the drive. Stopping once to glance across at the remaining pile of stones for the memorial. After a number of precise steps he stopped again. Inside the cage he would have been turning by now.

In a nice touch, Joe Phillips dropped a hand onto his shoulder to guide him the rest of the way.

You'll have to ride in the back with Stein, he said. Hope that's okay.

The border collie's sides shook with excitement. It yelped and hung its sloppy pink tongue over the edge of the truck.

I didn't want to spend another minute in the hotel, with its damp, complicated air. I didn't want to think about the reappearance of the key. It was a hopeless place to be, stuck between what I had seen and what I didn't know.

No one objected when I jumped up onto the tray of the truck.

By now Mole had dragged himself across to sit with his back to the cab, next to a small holding pen. He looked up to a sky floating beyond the driveway elms. He was no longer the wild man that had assaulted Uncle Warwick. His eyes were softened by all that blue expanse.

As soon as the truck began to move he looked across at me. You knew, he said.

No, I said. I had no idea.

But even I found it hard to believe. I was the hotelier's nephew. As far as the strangers were concerned, my world and that of the hotel were one and the same. The key belonged to the world that I was in.

I thought of all the times Doctor had asked about the key and all the times I had told him, confidently, sincerely, I was sorry. There was no news.

As we bumped out to the road Mole asked, And the woman in the hat? Is she a lie as well?

I don't know, I said.

Have you seen her?

No, I said.

It was the worst kind of news. Mole closed his eyes.

On our way through town he sat with his back pressed to the cab, his hands placed flat on the tray. To anyone in the street he might have been a seasonal worker brought in to pick corn.

I chose to stand, to keep my distance from him. Stein was there as well, and I was glad of that.

Mole held up a hand to shield his eyes. The sunstrike on the windows in town was too bright. He had to turn away. At the same time he straightened up and looked with interest at the people—kids on bikes, rattling by on skateboards, on their phones, others getting in and out of cars. People walking along, in no hurry.

We slowed down for the traffic to get around the large boulder still in the middle of the road. A number of kids stood on it pretending to direct traffic. What good mimics they were of our pompous instincts.

In the countryside the air smelt of pine and paddock and silage. Mole was interested in everything that flashed by. His wild hair swept his face. The breeze had a flattening effect on his features.

I remembered in Bill Francis's plane feeling pleasantly separated from my old life. But, on the back of the farm truck, I was returned to the general unpopulated airiness of it, the sheer volume of dumbness leaked by the hills and the inexhaustible determination of the sky not to think.

The last of the storm rain had only recently stopped and the river road was glassy with puddles. We bumped and splashed the rest of the way to the flooded edge of the river. Its turbulent surface was in a rush to reach somewhere, perhaps still unknown to itself. On the far side of it, stood hundreds of marooned sheep.

A number of men were already up to their waists in the river. They formed a human chain, each one of them as silent as a pitchfork, their faces at full strain. The men riding with

Joe Phillips spilled from the truck—and Mole joined them—to plunge unthinkingly into the cold current. Most of them threw up a hand and swore. A few, including Mole, were more stoic and waded in as if the shock of the water was nothing they hadn't experienced before.

I would have followed but a hand landed on my shoulder.

Not you, Joe Phillips said.

I shrugged out from under his hand.

Your uncle, he said. Listen, why don't you jump in the driver's seat? You can keep an eye on the stranger from there.

Well, that made sense. That's what I would be doing right now back at the hotel.

In the river, Mole was just another pair of hands for each sheep to be passed to. On this side of the river the rescued sheep clattered up the bank. Even though it was men who had saved them, they fled at the sight of us.

Joe stood on the back of the truck yelling and whistling instructions to Stein. And, on the far bank, the dog ran from one side of the mob to the other. Some of the sheep dug in but then, barked at, they plunged into the river and suddenly the rest had the urge to follow. Joe Phillips's instructions grew louder and more urgent. The dog had to race around to drive them back from the water. A number of sheep looked confused.

One at a time, you dumb fuck! Joe Phillips yelled at the dog.

The day was petering out. A weak sun occupied a far corner of the sky. I stayed in the cab until the hills turned dark. The last of the light dragged a shadow across the river. The men sank from view, and pretty soon all that could be seen were the glowing red eyes of the sheep.

I got down from the cab and gathered driftwood. A couple

of fires on the bank brought the faces of the men in the river back into view, along with the sheep, and their thin ragged upside-down legs. A sense of delicacy stuck to their snouts, as if they were aware they had an audience.

I warmed myself by the fire. Every now and then there was a tumble of rock and loose stones when one of the men climbed out to warm himself, and again when he stumbled back down the riverbank into the current. I waited for Mole. But he didn't take a turn by the fire.

'Come to me, Caroline!' one man yelled as he entered the water.

'Not if you were the last man alive!' yelled another voice from the river, and several others cheered and applauded.

Then night returned to the fast-moving current. A grunt lifted off it, the colic throat of a sheep. Some of the men let rip when they lost their footing and got their dry bits wet.

At a late hour, coffee gingered up with whisky crossed the river in a flask. After that, a few gleeful voices sang out. The comedians told jokes. The lonely hearted turned morose.

I slept—or thought I did—wrapped around the gear stick in the front of the truck.

I was up in time to see a filmy light in the east creep down from the hillsides. A dark litter in the sky as the flock changed course. Then a large yellow disc rose above the ridge, and, shortly after it, a light with more weight to it landed on the river with such force that every man standing in the water turned to look for his neighbour. All at once they began to talk. What a hell of a night it had been. They swore at the cold water. They swore at the bloody sheep they had grabbed arse up instead of by the head. No one appeared to give the stranger a second look, or seemed to care who he was.

At the hotel, I would be at the window about now, and, back in warmer days, up in time to see Doctor playing the hose over Mole.

I saw the stranger wobbling in the current, battling to stay awake. A wet ewe landed against his chest and his eyes bulged. They closed again the moment he passed the animal on, and his chin fell against his chest.

The man beside him yelled in his ear and Mole's head popped up again, his hands and arms spread, to receive the next animal.

This time he was knocked off balance, and the current swept him and the large ewe in his arms downriver. It was a strange and bewildering sight. The wet plastered head of the stranger drifted towards the bend with the fretful head of the sheep gazing back over the human shoulder.

The ewe began to struggle, but without much conviction. The stranger got an arm free and with his elbow struck it over the head, and they floated on.

Then Joe Phillips got in the truck to give chase. On a high bend, where the river twists back towards the hills, we waved and yelled, but without any effect, and so we drove on, skidding and fishtailing in the gravel.

On the river flats we braked, slid in the gravel. Joe kicked open his door and jumped out. From the back he got a coil of rope, and he ran across a paddock to the water's edge.

At the right moment he landed the rope on the current. Mole got a hand free to reach out, and when he managed to grab hold of it, without losing control of the ewe, we all cheered.

Joe Phillips hauled them in to the bank, and another farm-hand stepped into the shallows to take possession of the sheep. At its release Mole's arms flew up and he fell backwards into the river. In the fast water he rolled over and over, banging against the boulders until, in a channel of deeper water, he was able to reach out and grab a fistful of riverbank. The river pulled at his legs. He held on and then, seeing no one raced to his aid, he began to claw his way out.

On the dry ground he reeled about, stumbling like a drunk.

I thought he might try to run away. Instead, he looked up and saw the truck, and started towards it.

We leaned against the back of the truck—Joe Phillips, the farmhand and I. It might be winter, but the morning sun had surprising power. There was no wind. I had to unbutton the corduroy jacket. I would have taken it off if I didn't fear leaving it behind.

The stranger reported before us. His soaked shirt sleeves twisted around his wrists. His trousers sagged down beneath his belly button.

Good work, Joe said to him. I thought you'd lost her.

I helped Joe heave the ewe up into the truck. What a day that sheep was having. In the river one moment. Now on a dais raised like a trophy animal.

Joe stepped back and groaned when he saw how effing wet the ewe had made his effing shirtfront. He left me in charge of the sheep, and Mole, while he dug around in the front of the truck for a dry shirt. He peeled off the wet one, bunched it in his hand and looked for somewhere to toss it. Ended up throwing it at Mole who caught it.

It's yours if you want it, Joe said.

Mole gazed at the unexpected gift in his hands.

Joe yelled an instruction at Stein and the dog jumped up onto the tray, and growled. The ewe turned and trotted inside the holding pen.

Mole hauled himself after, a bit like the way he had from the river, and followed the ewe inside the pen, to lie where countless slain sheep had, each with its collar of dried blood.

There was enough room in the front but I told Joe Phillips I would ride in the back. I told him I should keep an eye on the stranger.

We left the river and drove up onto the smooth tarseal. The panting ewe leaned against the side of the pen and absorbed the bumps on slanted legs. The dog lay flat and watchful on the tray, resting its head on its paws.

A shadow lifted off a hill and a gasp of sunlight spooked a mob of sheep. The hillside trembled as they fled down the stony slopes as if intent on galloping out of their skins.

How quickly everything could change—as though the one thing was forever waiting for the other to turn up. Two dogs— as sleek as black wire—snapped at the heels of the scattering sheep on the hill. It was a magnificent sight.

In town, people were on their way to work. Shops were opening. Mr Hughes was putting out his trays of fruit. It was a gorgeous morning for tennis.

A woman bent down to kiss the head of a boy who had a school satchel strapped to his back. The stranger made a feeble attempt to get her attention.

As we flew by, the woman smiled and waved. So did the boy. And Mole, who had looked foolishly hopeful, sank down in the pen, threw back his head and closed his eyes.

And now it seemed that whatever might have happened had passed. A more familiar world closed around us—the elms, the pebbly driveway, the stem of smoke from the fire in the hotel foyer rising above the grey slates.

We lurched to a halt outside the hotel. Joe Phillips came around to the back of the truck to open the holding pen. Stein jumped down onto the drive. At a shout from the farmhand the dog leapt back onto the tray. It moved to block the sheep, then it barked at the stranger. Mole got the message and began to back his way out of the pen.

Uncle Warwick was at the door. Viktor, too, ready with a broom handle.

The soaked stranger started towards the hotel entrance but Uncle Warwick spread his arms, and the kitchenhand used the broom handle as a prod to redirect him around the side.

In the backyard the stranger slowed down—as was to be expected. His face was a bit broken up but it still managed to be thrilled by the little things. Sunshine, for example, which lit up the russet ivy growing on the side of the garden wall, and if he'd cared to look he might have noticed the green heads in the vegetable patch. The windows above shone. One of them was open and someone happened to be singing. The same sunlight landed hard on the floor of the cage where Doctor lay on his side over the plate warmer. I had an idea it must have been left on all night.

I had never seen so many flies. Lines of flies, all of them tracking to Doctor's filthy arse.

Doctor was flyblown, despite the cold conditions, and that information hit Mole so forcefully that he rushed to the cage, and stood impatiently while Uncle Warwick unlocked the gate.

Doctor's body shook and trembled. The smell of rotting flesh was dreadful.

The gate opened and Mole burst through. He knelt beside Doctor and tried to get him into a sitting position. But as Doctor's head flopped against his chest, Mole let him go.

He looked up at the window where the singing had come from. His face was red from the cold of the river. But his eyes. They would have scared a small child.

He struggled to his feet like a man swaying in a storm, and he bellowed out a list of demands.

Clean water, food, dry clothing, beds, food.

The window went on shining brightly.

Viktor threw in a bowl of scraps, which enraged Mole. He swore at the kitchenhand, but he couldn't help himself. He bent down to pick up a piece of celery in his raw hands. His mouth opened. But instead of swallowing or chewing he looked across to Doctor. Again he knelt down beside the mud-caked rags. He had to brush the flies away before he could push the celery against Doctor's crusted lips. The grim line of Doctor's mouth refused to part, but Mole persisted, gently pushing with the celery until at last the mouth opened. Mole put in the celery, but Doctor let it fall out.

Mole spat on his finger to clean the celery, put it inside his own mouth and chewed until it was pulpy. Once more he waved the flies away. This time he jemmied a finger inside Doctor's mouth. Uncle Warwick grunted with approval, and returned to the hotel.

I stayed put. I was glad to have the strangers for the distraction they provided. Inside the hotel there would be no avoiding the subject of the key.

I watched Mole pick at the scraps in the dirt. The flies returned. More and more flies—an incredible number really—drifting towards Doctor's rear end.

One small puddle still glistened inside the cage. Mole cupped his hands in it to splash water over Doctor's infected area. He repeated the exercise. Each time he released the water, flies rose from the sodden rags.

Katie yelled across the yard that the breakfast sausages were ready.

I wished she hadn't. At the news of the sausages Mole looked up. It was as though a piece of his old life had been granted to him.

Tell Viktor I'll be up there in a second, I said.

He said they'll go cold.

I will be up in a second, I said!

I had to chase her back inside and up the stairs. This time I didn't return to the backyard. I couldn't face Mole.

From the landing I watched Mole roll Doctor onto his stomach and begin to feel around the fly-infested area.

It was filthy work and Mole used the puddle to wash his hands. He was careful about it. Using his clean hand to scoop up the water, he took care not to pollute the puddle. Instead, he plunged his filthy fingers into the mud, letting the dirt do the cleansing. I believe there is some science to support that idea.

My sausages were waiting, but I stayed at the window.

Inside the cage, Mole's wandering eye caught up with a piece of carrot. He picked it up out of the mud. Held it between thumb and forefinger and nibbled at the clean part.

The flies returned. A cloud of them, visible even from the

distance of the window.

Mole looked across the pen. There was a wet patch of mud where the puddle had been.

Katie's piping voice rose from behind the door. Viktor says he will feed the sausages to the animals unless you come upstairs right now.

Mole knelt down to part the back of Doctor's trousers, then he undid his own flies and belt. His trousers fell around his ankles. He held his cock, took aim at doctor's fly-infested area, and urinated.

32

Then what? Mr Hughes wanted to know.

Then I dashed off to eat the sausages. So I am not in a position to say.

I answered the rest of their questions as best I could. For instance, during his night in the river, did I sense in the stranger a temptation, however brief, to escape?

No, I said.

Who can say what passes in another's thoughts?

No, I said again.

But, to my surprise, flight had occurred to me. It was as the truck bumped along the shingle river road, I had unexpectedly smelt a new freedom and possibility for myself. I wonder if it was the un-anchoring effect of the open air. And, I was tired after a night in the truck. Without inviting or fishing for such a thought I had closed my eyes and imagined I was in someone else's vehicle, a vehicle I had hitched a ride in. It was going somewhere. Towards hills. Across a plain. It was the feeling of movement—rather than any detail. The moment seemed to be some time in the future. Then the truck had braked and my eyes had popped open—and there across the flats, I picked up Mole, bobbing along in the river with the ewe in his arms.

The mess out there, said Uncle Warwick. They've completely ruined the backyard. Honestly, it's a pigsty.

Time is nature's great healer, said Mr Wooten.

Try explaining that to the guests, replied my uncle.

There aren't any guests at present—and that thought seemed to circulate the room.

An absolute pigsty, repeated Warwick. The grass has all gone, you know. Sport?

Yes, that's right, I said. The grass has worn away completely.

The Trustees were as they have been on other occasions—sympathetic. It is quite incredible what the strangers are prepared to tolerate. But it is also an indication of the immense value they attach to their experience, that they continue to refuse to share it.

And what about the key?

No one around the table seemed interested. It was a strange thing to witness, like we were all standing on a melting icefloe but none of us had the courage to say anything.

I would have said we were trapped—trapped by what we could not say.

Until someone spoke up.

Should we be doing this?

The room went quiet, as each Trustee seemed to check in with himself that, God forbid, he wasn't the source of that comment.

Who else but the wayward Mr Byrd?

One or two began to laugh. Mr Byrd's smile grew more and more unsteady. After all, we now have the key, he said. He looked up hopefully.

The key was lost, and then it was found. That is the correct

197

way to describe it, said Uncle Warwick.

Mr Byrd continued. Yes, and good on you, Warwick, for coming up with it.

My uncle laid the same wary eye on Mr Byrd as he had on Joe Phillips's dog out the front of the hotel.

I would like to respond to that question, said Mr Bennett. We have come this far. There is reason to believe that we are winning and that the will of the strangers is starting to weaken. Hopefully, soon they will see reason. But to drop the ball at this stage—well, it would be irresponsible. We have a responsibility to ourselves and to this town and its people. And, yes, the work is unpleasant. But that is not an argument.

A murmur of assent from around the table.

Mr Byrd raised a hand. That's not what I meant, he began.

Yes, interrupted the chair. I know. We have the key, and a whole new bargaining chip. Especially now that the younger stranger has had a taste of freedom.

I raised my hand to get Mr Bennett's attention.

Should I be taking any of us this down?

Heavens no, he replied, and almost laughed aloud at my naivety. We're just thinking aloud.

Then he was struck by a new thought. He held his head on its side. He seemed to be listening for the right words to come to him.

You can say this, however. We are close. We were getting somewhere until the weather closed in.

The Trustees rose as one, grateful for the subject of the weather. There were new breaches of the river, more food damage to report and share. Amazing new sights. A dead sheep had been found in the lower branches of a tree, and a woman's dress was found wrapped around a car aerial. On it went until, at last, the voices ran out of air, and it was Uncle Warwick who brought everyone back to the topic.

I believe the memorial is nearly finished, he said, and he looked down the table to check with me. He spoke in the same calm manner as he did after Mole punched him.

It will depend on the weather, I said. And with winter on its way.

Winter's practically here now, observed Mr Fish.

Well, let's say spring at the latest, said Uncle Warwick.

At the absolute latest, confirmed the chair.

You can put that down, he instructed.

No one stayed for drinks. I was the last to leave. I listened to their feet crossing the foyer to the door. A moment later car headlights strafed the windows. I wanted to think more about what had been said and, more to the point, what hadn't been said. No one had questioned my uncle about the key. We had simply proceeded with the agenda. Now I wondered if I had missed something. I wondered if the conversation I expected to hear had already occurred, on the night I was at the river.

It was dark. The dying light bulbs in the chandelier blinked and burned. The hotel sounded empty. It creaked and groaned. And the creaking was the sound of something broken.

I found Uncle Warwick cleaning the Gents, mopping furiously, all his attention on the gleaming tiles, as if that was where virtue lay. He looked angry. The skin around his ruffled dark eyebrows was red as he put all his effort into the mop.

He was aware of my presence but went on mopping, as if he knew what was coming and hoped to forestall the moment. When he finally stopped he was slightly out of breath.

I had intended to ask where the key had been found. But at the last second I couldn't bear to. I knew he would tell a lie which, as soon as I heard it, would bind me to it and then I would inherit the deceit.

But what to do? I could not think quickly enough.

I know what fear can do. I'd felt it in Bill Francis's plane that time we lifted off. For a second or two I was required to believe that the plane could occupy the air like a windblown dandelion does. Only slowly and gradually had I released the fear, a bit at a time, to the view spreading below.

The opportunity to speak was gone in a second.

As Uncle Warwick turned his attention back to the mop, I yelled at the back of his head. We have to let them out!

Warwick leaned the mop against the wall. Sport, he said.

But I went on. Doctor is sick, I said. He needs help. We need to let them go.

Yes, he said slowly. One eye hitched a bit higher than the other. I did not think he was agreeing with me but with something else that had crossed his mind. Possibly something to do with my father.

I thought Mr Bennett made a pretty good fist of explaining our position, he said. Earlier in the evening, you were there, Sport. Tell me if I am wrong, by all means. But I thought everyone understood.

He spoke slowly and warily in case I was to spring at him like Mole had.

If you look in your minutes, I think you will find that the Trust as a whole has agreed on the next course of action.

And the key? I asked.

His face cheered up.

Ah yes, he said. You won't believe it. The key was in my bloody trouser pocket. The ones I wore when we were building the cage. The fly broke and I gave them to Dawn to fix. They've been sitting in a pile next to her sewing machine all this time.

He shook his head at the wonder of it, and I was almost convinced.

33

The sky is ragged this morning. It looks tired. Patches of it are loaded with some dismal faraway event.

Mr Wooten, hat in hand, has come to explain to the strangers that although the Trust is now in possession of the key—and yes, yes, thank goodness they can now lay their hands on it for whenever it might be needed—most likely when the memorial is finished and the words have been supplied.

Mr Wooten meant to be encouraging, but when he stopped he seemed aware only of the wintry air and a need to put his hat back on.

Doctor lay in the mud, arms spread—possibly unconscious. Mole stood against the cage, with a stupefied expression. I expected him to fly into rage. But when Mr Wooten popped his hat back on to indicate the meeting was over, Mole slipped from view behind the stone wall. I had a feeling his legs had buckled under him.

I picked up the clarinet and began to play. I wanted to lift the spirits of the strangers. But after a while it was too cold to have the window open. Once or twice a year the fence wires on the farm used to glisten with ice, and voices carried surprisingly far in the thin air.

With the window closed, I played louder, but I doubt Doctor heard anything through the walls of sleep.

We still want to help and to show our compassion—and that would have been abundantly clear to anyone who saw Mole put his filthy hand through the feeding hole for Dawn to rub it warm between her own palms. Selflessly rubbing warmth into the same hand that had plunged into Doctor's fly-infested arse.

I hurried upstairs to stand on the toilet seat, by then I could hear Dawn telling Katie not to point, it is rude, the lump in the mud is not dead, and she shouldn't talk like that. The lump has ears. It can hear.

Dawn emptied a small bag onto the grass beneath the feeding hole—dried fruit, biscuits, a few bananas.

I don't like it here, Katie said. It stinks.

Her mother began to tell her off, but Mole stopped her.

The girl is right. It does stink. It is good to hear the truth spoken again.

On the landing I met Dawn and Katie coming up the stairs. Before I had a chance to say anything, Dawn said brightly, Now, if you know anything about your uncle then you will know how forgetful he is.

Fine, I said. But don't you think we should let them out?

Yes, she said simply, and she looked up at me with a faint smile.

The girl went on banging the toe of her shoe into the step of the stairs.

Then why haven't we let them out?

Dawn's smile grew more confident. It was the kind of smile

a teacher reserves for the class idiot.

I said, What about bringing them inside the hotel? Their old room is free.

She turned her attention to the toe-banging noise on the stairs.

Come on, young lady. It's time you had a bath.

No, said the girl. I don't want a bath. I want to feed the strangers.

Katie waited to be told she couldn't, then she turned to me. Viktor dropped one of your sausages on the floor, she said, then he picked it up and put it back on the plate. He said he'd throw me out the window if I told you.

Are you afraid? I asked her.

No.

Katie is right. The smell is dreadful. I have to tip out the wheelbarrow as fast as I can. But I also have to pack the stones. Where am I to get a fresh breath from? There is no choice other than to get used to the stench. And the surprising thing is, you do.

I'm working above the matted head of Doctor. His eyes are closed, and he doesn't move. Actually, but for the flies, I wouldn't have known he was there.

Mole is keeping a watch on me from the log. His eye will not let go of me. I don't know what to make of it. It's as though a plan has been hatched that I am yet to be advised of. Or he wishes I was someone else. Or he wishes me to remember. But remember what? For now, I am the one making their home more comfortable.

The stone wall on one side is now up to my chest. My plan

is to go higher. I don't want to see into the cage anymore.

There is a depressing development I need to bring to the attention of the Trustees. It is almost a waste of time to speak of the strangers in the plural anymore.

Doctor has fallen by the wayside. Mostly he is asleep, or unconscious. I'm not even sure he gets up to urinate. He lies on his side, one eye flicks open as he reaches to see if the plate warmer is on. Then it closes.

This afternoon, returning with another wheelbarrow-load from the front of the hotel, I found Viktor and Mole arguing over the hose.

Its use is embargoed until further notice. It is for the sake of the strangers' comfort. There is already too much water in the pen. In a downpour it is subject to flooding, and their little vegetable garden also faces ruin if the hose is used indiscriminately.

I heard the kitchenhand say, I'm sorry, but those are the rules.

The news seemed to make Viktor lighter, more engaged, as if at last the world is taking notice of him.

He pours the tea and passes the cups through the feeding hole.

Careful, he says cheerfully. You don't want to burn yourselves. And the carrots and celery, were they okay?

Mole doesn't answer. Instead he tries to help Doctor up, and to get him to sip his tea, but it is hopeless. Tea dribbles down his chin. Doctor's dead eyes stare ahead.

Doctor urgently requires medical attention. A sheep with flystrike is gone the moment it lies down; it is on its way to a slow and painful death. Its sides tremble and its eyes dim into a place deep inside itself where the flies lay their eggs.

Doctor is not quite at that stage, but he is well on his way—in my opinion.

At breakfast, Uncle Warwick weighed up what I had to say.

I had to remind him that Doctor had volunteered to look at Katie's arm and that he correctly diagnosed the fracture. Without his input she may not have gone to hospital, I said.

Well in that case, Sport, he will know, won't he? He will know not to place himself in danger because, after all, he is a doctor.

If he is a doctor, I said.

Didn't you just say he was?

As you know, Doctor is more of a nickname. We could call him Napoleon but it wouldn't make him Napoleon.

Around and around in circles we went.

Doctor has been muttering in his sleep, I said.

My uncle showed more interest.

Just the one word, so far, I said. 'Bath'.

When he is asleep?

Yes. He sleeps nearly all the time. But that's what a sheep with flystrike will do as well.

A bath, you say? He seemed to consider the idea.

They have rejected so many things we've offered, he said. Remember the clothes? They didn't even get them out of the packets. You remember that. It was embarrassing to return those gifts to donors. I could see them wondering what kind of ship we run here?

But a bath, I said. It isn't such a big thing to ask for.

Uncle Warwick squeezed his eyes shut to think. Tell you

what, he said. You decide.

At last I could provide Doctor with something he wanted. A bath! It was almost the air that the raptor seeks. The old life back. A renewal of sensation. The skin alive again, pink, covered in suds.

I was excited and happy. I had news for Doctor. Wonderful news. I stood on my toes and spread my arms along the top of the stone wall to look for him in the mud. His head faced away from me.

I had to ask Mole to turn him over so he could hear and respond to my good news.

To the matted hair and fly-buzzed eyes I said, I have an offer. You may have a bath.

He did not respond.

I asked Mole, Is he sleeping?

He ignored the question. A bath, you said?

Yes. A hot bath. Or a warm bath, if that is preferred. Hot may be too hot, if you know what I mean.

I do, nodded Mole. But a bath will not fit inside the cage. We cannot accommodate a bath. As you can see, our place is filled with furnishings. I doubt there is room for a bath.

This is what rubs my uncle up the wrong way. Everything Mole says arrives with the barb of sarcasm. And when Mole chooses to be silent, the barb settles in his eye.

The bath is inside the hotel, as you well know, I said.

Yes, he said without much enthusiasm. But it will mean leaving the cage.

We looked down at Doctor. A cloud of flies lifted and rose past his nose, then fell according to a swelling motion in the air detectable only to themselves.

Of course his clothes will need to be removed, I said. I can arrange for them to be washed.

Mole seemed more interested, so I explained to him that although the hot water will kill any eggs and maggots in his clothing, Uncle Warwick will require him to have a preliminary scrub with the hose before he enters the hotel. No offence intended.

You mentioned an offer? he said.

But before I could answer, another voice was heard, startling us both. It was as if the mud was speaking

No! it cried. And, Doctor's exhausted head fell back.

34

We lost at tennis later that evening. Weirdly my uncle didn't care. We crept up the hotel drive, parked, and switched off the headlights. And as Warwick stayed put behind the wheel, I let go of the door handle and settled into my seat.

Why, he asked, would he reject the bath? Why refuse kindness when it is offered?

At a guess I would have said Doctor was asserting his will. But that's not what I said—a shared bewilderment seemed the safest approach.

I don't know, I said.

The silence in the car hardened. My uncle stared ahead.

Your father was like that, he said. As stubborn as a fucking mule. Someone had to tell him it was raining before he would notice. Remember that business with the goats? I could have told him it would never work.

Did you?

No. Course not. He wouldn't have listened. I never met anyone more stubborn.

Well, we can agree on that much. My father's life now seems like one long act of wilful resistance. Selling up the house in suburbs and moving to the country. Giving up friends and neighbours he liked for the great echoing silence of the hills. Secretly warring against a foe known only to himself.

As for Doctor, said my uncle. I was quite prepared to open the cage. With Viktor's help we could have gotten him up the stairs and ready for a bath.

He fell silent—we both did—at the thought of undressing the stranger. Peeling those filthy rags off him.

Come on, let's get out of here, he said. The door on my uncle's side opened.

Inside the hotel the creaking floorboards made us step more lightly. It was as if we were sneaking in. Then Uncle Warwick stopped. Cocked his head, ran back to the door and swung it open. A guest might have been outside. Instead, the night rocked in the doorway. Uncle Warwick shook his head.

I thought I heard someone, he said. As he walked to his office, his hotelier's substance seemed to spill from him. Without a guest, who was he? He squeezed himself around the reception desk and into his small office. He closed the door after him.

I heard him and Dawn arguing later that night. It was a new noise in the hotel. And an ugly one.

The stone walls are nearly finished. That's my good news for the Trustees. I can report that the strangers now inhabit a space more resembling a pen than a cage.

And the difference?

The pen has a wintering-over atmosphere, I explain.

More comfortable, do you mean? asks Mr Bennett.

I would think so.

But how would I know? How would anyone know? I am making it up.

Years ago at the beach I had to use a piece of driftwood to haul a pig's head out of a rolling shorebreak. On the wet shingle its eyes were slits, like Doctor's. And, like the stranger, it looked fed up with its situation. It had been eaten by lice. And the lice still had a fair way to go.

The noise of the flies is constant in the backyard. I can hear them on the other side of the pen as I work. They have no interest in me or Mole.

This morning, though, as I placed the first rock of the day, Doctor came alive. I think it was the sound the stone made. It was like disturbing a lizard. His eyelids flickered and drew back and his pale eyes held the sky—and briefly, foolishly, I thought every conversation under the sun would now be possible, at last, including the offer of the bath, and it would be like the old days when we used to discuss music, and other things. But, then his eyelids closed, his head fell back into the filth, and I was left holding a rock.

The truck fantasy keeps coming back to me. I am on my way somewhere, and the feeling of relief is real. The wind is rushing past me. I am on the back of that truck. And, at last, I am going. I am on my way. But the fantasy never moves on. I never appear to arrive anywhere. The fantasy only places me on the back of the truck. Where I am, I have no idea. But the feeling, unmistakably, is one of exhilaration.

It comes on in the shower. And several times now I have lost my way on the clarinet. I am back on the truck without any idea of how I got there.

Even now, as I piss dreamily into the upstairs toilet, I am on the truck. Then I come to. The naked light bulb. The gleaming walls. The tight elbowy space. And I think, since I'm here, I might as well jump up on the toilet to see if the strangers are awake. I open the window, feel the cold blast. It is almost light. The faint voice is Doctor's. It is almost a whisper.

'Inside me. Cicadas.'

I think that's what he said. Cicadas.

Then, 'People…scattering…like pigeons. Has there been another bomb scare?'

His clarity is back. It is the old Doctor emerging out of his creaturely skin of mud and shit.

I wonder if I should run down there and renew the offer of a bath?

'The wallpaper,' he says. Then he groans. 'The cicadas are back.'

Flies, he must mean. Although at this hour I would not have thought so. He must mean the maggots inside him.

Then he sits up so unexpectedly I knock my head on the window.

The moon slips behind a cloud, and the strangers recede.

Just Doctor's voice, now.

'Foxgloves I said to her one time. Foxgloves.'

That was all. Doctor went quiet.

Mole cups his hand behind Doctor's matted head. I expect he is about to give him a drink from the hose. The embargo has been lifted.

Mole had hauled a length of the hose inside the cage. The strangers seem to be more entwined, more caring. Mole is sitting with Doctor's head resting against his chest. His knees cradle the older stranger. Then he straightens his shoulders and pulls on the hose. And the hose, I see, is around Doctor's neck. Mole's elbows are high and they shake with the effort. As he throws his head back I can hear him grunting. 'Come on,' he says. 'Come on.' It is unclear who he is urging—himself or Doctor. Doctor's legs kick. The tips of his feet shake. His hands clutch at the air. They clutch and they clutch. Then they both fall backwards. Doctor in the arms of Mole. The hose still wrapped around his neck, and his head on Mole's chest but at an odd angle, like it's been half torn from his shoulders.

Mole wriggles free. His head drops and his long hair falls forward. For the moment he looks like a man praying. Then he presses a hand down on Doctor's chest to wearily push himself onto his feet. He draws a breath. Slaps one side of his face, then the other.

The spade is leaning against the mesh. He hurries for it. Grabs the handle and begins to dig.

He works quickly.

He stops once, and holds his head absolutely still—the sound of a toilet flushing passes—his head drops and he angles the spade back into the earth.

Dirt lands on dirt. A sticking and splashy sound.

The slack hose is in the mud near the log.

Doctor's corpse.

The practical steps.

The stranger swings the spade, and heaves soil to each side of the deepening trench. He's up to his knees now.

There is a distressing dumbness to everything in the back-yard—the ivy, the garden wall, the unloved swing, the stones, the finches in the long grass. I am amazed to discover I still have the presence of mind to note that the grass needs cutting.

The trench is up to Mole's waist. He tosses the spade aside, crawls out, picks Doctor up by the shoulders and, as the morning light strikes the dead man's exhausted face, drags his bare feet through the mud. At the side of the trench Mole lets go of Doctor's shoulders, then goes back for the moccasin and boot parked by the log. These he lobs into the grave. Mole slips the toe of his boot under Doctor's knees to swing the older man's legs into the hole. One hand seems to claw the ground before the rest of him topples over the edge.

The pipes of the hotel start to gurgle. There is still some tidying up to do. Some of the shitting soil to drag across, and some of the grave soil to drag the other way and pat down until the mud is all of a kind.

I stare for a long time at what I have seen. I stare at the dirt. I can't take my eyes off the dirt. The dirt grew into the day. It grew larger. The sun found the rusted swing. It rose against the windows, lifted the mesh off the pen, and returned me to the rich soil. The sun moved again and this time the grass leapt up. All horribly bright. The shadow moved off the stone rabbit.

There's a kind of peaceful aliveness in dead faces. Where had I read that? Or heard it. Probably from Mr Thorn. I remembered Edith's head lying in the long grass like a battered suitcase. And, my father's hysteria. But I did not feel any of that now. I was cold, as if all emotion had been squeezed out of me. Later, I would wonder why and how that happened. But, for now, I knew who or what I was. I was that stone rabbit. I had ears. But they did not hear. I had eyes. But they did not see.

I had a strong urge to smash the window. I struggled to get dressed. My clothes disgusted me. And at the sight of my father's corduroy jacket I burst into tears.

I should tell someone. Yes. Of course. I should.

The question. What is the question? The question is this. At what point did I know what was going to happen? The second question. Why did I not do anything to prevent it?

35

There is one week in the year in the country when it is impossible to escape the bellowing of cows. It is after the trucks have come and taken away their calves. The noise is tremendous—a trumpeting to bring down the sky. Mum used to go and stay at the hotel during that week. She said she couldn't sleep with that racket going on in the hills. But it soon passes—the grieving, the loss.

Within a week, the beasts resume their lonely lives, crawling across the hills. Or they lie down and drop their heads into the grass. The hills push back. Some awful accommodation is offered that at first everyone resists, then welcomes.

And that is how it was. The stranger sat on the log, his legs folded under him, and he waited for his breakfast.

I got down off the toilet seat. I spent a moment on the landing to compose. It dawned on me that I could not tell anyone, not without implicating myself. I'd done nothing to prevent Mole strangling Doctor. At the time, it hadn't occurred to me to intervene. And now I could not escape the thought that, by doing nothing, a part of me had held one end of the hose.

I find Viktor in the kitchen, in his chef's outfit, check pants, a white jacket and white hat. The hotel has guests for a change, a touring cyclist couple who turned up late yesterday afternoon in goggles and lycra. I put them in a room with a view of the shops across the road.

Viktor is chopping parsley.

Let me give you a hand with the feeding out, I say. Here. I'll take the tray, shall I?

Two cups, I notice.

We step out onto the porch.

After you, Viktor.

I am relieved it is not just me and the stranger. I am glad to have this cushion between us.

Viktor takes great pains not to spill anything. So he doesn't look up until he has reached the side of the pen.

Doctor's not here, he says.

Mole looks to catch my eye. He is curious to know at what stage of the story I have placed myself. Was I at the window? What did I see? He can't be sure. He looks troubled, and that pleases me—for Doctor's sake.

Viktor puts down the slops. He grabs hold of the gate and gives it a shake.

The stranger turns away. There is an easing of tension in his face.

Now we have a routine to get through. Others must be allowed to catch up with what we already know.

Doctor, he's not here, observes Viktor again.

No, replies the stranger this time.

Well, Viktor says to him. Where did he go?

He didn't say, replies the stranger.

Confusion and anger cloud Viktor's face. This is not how it

is supposed to be. He is the one outside the cage. The cards are supposed to be in his favour.

Did you happen to hear anything last night? I say to Viktor. You know, anything suspicious?

He has to think.

No, he says.

Are you quite sure?

Yes, he replies, a little frightened now. This is bad, he says. This is very bad.

It is unclear who it is bad for.

He looks down at the pail of slops and the tray with the two cups sitting on the grass.

Warwick, he says. We need to tell your uncle.

Go ahead. I'll wait here.

Mole and I watch the kitchenhand run up the steps. The door into the hotel closes, but we continue to look in its direction.

I am reluctant to meet Mole's eye. He will look guilty and I will feel guilty for knowing why.

I would have said to the Trustees. I was just observing—doing my usual job.

So, says Mole, but nothing more. A shrug. And a gaze that ends near the top of the garden wall.

I want to look across at Doctor's grave. It is hard to believe he is down there in the ground. It smells. It smells of shit. Everything smells of shit.

Victor returns with my uncle. The news is big and startling. Uncle Warwick assumes the kitchenhand is wrong. If he keeps squinting at the ground inside the pen a sheet of shit will rise in the shape of Doctor.

It makes no sense, but the unsense of it is there to see. Doctor

218

is gone. He must have turned himself into mist and drifted away.

Christ, he says. Like Viktor, my uncle grabs the gate and gives it a shake.

More confidently now, the stranger returns to the log and sits on his hands.

Warwick places his face close to the mesh. His voice is calm, as if authority might still have a part to play. Who let Doctor out? he asks.

I am not aware that anyone did, replies Mole.

Then how did he get out?

I am unaware, says Mole.

I suppose he just wandered up to the shops and never returned, says Uncle Warwick.

Viktor is holding a boiled egg in his hand. Warwick, shall I give it to him?

No. Not just yet, Viktor.

What about the slops then? asks Viktor.

Warwick raises a hand for silence. He wants to concentrate on the stranger. Doctor must have shared his plan with you, he says.

He didn't speak of a plan, replies Mole. He did speak obsessively of the woman in the hat.

Uncle Warwick turns to me and I shake my head.

I slept through, I tell him. Then I add, I wasn't feeling well. Something I ate.

My uncle turns to Viktor.

He ate what I ate and you ate, Warwick. The mushroom-and-chicken pie, says Viktor.

This is getting us nowhere. Uncle Warwick switches his attention back to the stranger.

Tell me where Doctor went. And Viktor will give you the egg.

He did not say, replies the stranger. Now, can I please have the boiled egg?

So, he didn't say?

The stranger smiles down at his feet. It is clear the hotelier doesn't know the right questions to unlock the puzzle.

No, he replies. He did not say.

So how the hell did he get out?

I did not see him get out, replies the stranger.

Part of me relished the honesty of that answer.

Now can I have the egg? he asks.

It was a difficult moment to endure, to pretend ignorance—to, in effect, stand in the stranger's corner. That is what Mole must have seen. An unwilling ally perhaps, but one with a gag stuffed in his mouth. And later, when I recalled this conversation, it was like a shift in the weather—the wind blowing strongly in one direction, then changing to the other. All our smugness came blowing back into our faces.

I would very much like something to eat, says Mole. It has been such a long time since I had a proper meal. I remember, when we were first put in here, we were offered scrambled eggs and...

And what? asks Uncle Warwick.

That's all, says the stranger. I am too weak to say more.

Mole didn't have long to wait. Viktor returned with the tray. Suddenly it was like in the old days. He opened his mouth for Viktor to reach through the feeding hole with a spoonful of scrambled egg.

He finished the last spoonful and as he rose to full height he knocked into the mesh, and a number of loose stones clattered to the ground.

It was momentarily distracting for Uncle Warwick, and the stranger took full advantage.

You have the key, Mole said. The whole time you had the key.

Uncle Warwick did not so much as shift a hair. He did not appear to breathe.

Panic entered the stranger's face.

Please, he said. Please. I beg you.

Uncle Warwick suddenly looked satisfied.

Yes, of course, he said. As soon as Doctor returns we will be happy to release you both.

The position was so reasonably put that it was hard to argue with.

On our way back inside I let Uncle Warwick and Viktor go ahead.

Sausages, Viktor reminded me.

Yes. Yes. I'll be up in a minute.

I waited until I heard them muttering on the stairs.

The stranger got up from the log and walked to the side of the pen. I was reminded of the crow at the zoo, the way he peered, his expectant face narrowing back at me—with all kinds of dreamy possibilities. Could I now be counted on in a new way?

36

In the ledger is a series of drawings and doodles, and not just of lighthouses. I've done a diagram most days to chart the movements of the strangers. Now I wonder if I will bother. It is like a clock. You need two hands to make sense of it.

With Doctor gone, there is no need to refer to 'Mole' anymore. He has slipped back into 'the stranger', a castaway who spends his days alone on the log, examining his fingernails.

As a child I would scribble over a picture I didn't like.

Bill Francis once spoke of a bad storm that left his paddocks covered in dead lambs. He had to haul them into a pile, empty a can of petrol over the carcasses and then throw a match. A plume of flame hurried over the pile of corpses, looking for a way in. The two things, he said, seemed quite separate. The flame, the dead sheep. Then the flame burst into a dozen flames and fed on the bodies. For a day and a half, he said, they burned. The smell of burning wool hung about. The front windows of his gracious old house woke for weeks to a blackened patch of earth. Then the rains had come, and soon after, he said, he couldn't see where the pyre had been. By next season, lambs were happily nibbling grass over the bones of their siblings.

An early spring gale blew in the night after Mole buried Doctor. The wind tore through the backyard. In town the eyes of everyone seemed to be more alive. It howled all night and well into the afternoon. I closed the curtain and sat on my bed. I remembered wild days like this on the farm when whole hillsides seemed to catch fire.

It was gone by the next morning and I returned to my task with the memorial stones. I worked on the side closest to my window. I was determined to remove the cage from my view.

Mole got up from the log. All he could do was stare. We were shackled to things that could not be discussed.

Doctor was always the more reasonable one. We liked him better. The words for the memorial, if they were to come, the Trustees felt sure would have come from him.

So now I worked at a task that I doubted would ever be completed—yet I ran between the diminishing rock pile in front of the hotel and the backyard.

Night fell, and I worked on under a light left on in an upstairs window.

I could hear Mole shuffling along the inside wall, looking for a gap in the stones to see me.

His muffled voice appealed to me to switch on the plate warmer. I slapped down another stone. There was a pause. He said he understood it involved a cost, he said, but he would be most grateful if the hotelier and the Trust could agree on a short period, say between midnight and first light, during which the plate warmer could be turned on.

I finished the row, then stepped back from the wall and listened to his sniffle and mumbling. I could almost sense his ears twitching for my whereabouts. When I heard him scamper away from me I picked up the handles of the wheelbarrow and shook the loose stones, and his breathless movement hurried back to where I stood.

Please, he said, his voice rising. Please help me.

That night his screams were terrible. There was no Doctor to calm him down. No one to take him by the hand and guide him across the pen to the log, to sit him down and shake the nightmare out of him.

So the screams carried on.

I heard feet on the stairs. I sat up in bed and waited. The feet thumped their way back up the stairs. I heard Dawn shout at Uncle Warwick. A door was slammed.

The stranger went on screaming. In the end Viktor ran outside and turned on the hose.

37

Mr Hughes was first to resign. He said he couldn't give any more time to the Trust. His business was suffering and he had nothing left to contribute.

Mr Wooten followed a few days later. He had enjoyed his time on the Trust and believed in its vision but what we had sought to bring forward had, in his view, slipped back, which was rather disappointing.

Mr Fish didn't turn up to the meeting and later that evening, when Uncle Warwick asked me to ring him, the line was dead.

Mr Byrd turned up in person to tell Uncle Warwick his heart was no longer in it. When my uncle asked whether he would like a peep out the window at my stonework he burst out with, 'For Christ's sake Warwick, what the hell is the matter with you?' and made for the door.

Mr Bennett made noises about winding up the Trust before he disappeared inside the warren of management running the dam upriver.

Dawn was the last to go. She and my uncle had terrible rows. She demanded he hand over the key. He hid it from her. She told him to open the cage and let Mole go or she was leaving.

A few days later I stood at an upstairs window and watched her walk to the waiting car holding Katie's hand and clutching suitcases. Dawn's brother-in-law got out. A tall slim man in jeans with a long grey ponytail.

He held the back door open. Dawn pushed Katie in first, then followed her.

Uncle Warwick came out to the drive. He might have been seeing off a guest except that he was in his slippers. He closed the door, then tapped the roof of the car, and it reversed down the drive.

In their various ways they all sank into the hotel's past.

When I go across the road to pick up bananas for the stranger, Mr Hughes's thin smile does not extend far. He does not want to pry into that world he was once part of.

The other day as we passed in the street Mr Byrd looked away and coughed into his hand.

I might as well be water passing in the gutter.

At night I get out the ledger, open a day at random and read the Trustees' comments. Who were these people who gave their considered opinions and are now nowhere to be found?

My job at the window is over. My eyes have been returned to me. I remember the descent of the plane and the land jolting into view. The land that from the air my father had once dreamily thought of as 'our future' had to be walked across, and what I had taken as smooth from the air, a delicately worked-out quilt, turned out to be rough and pot-holed, and covered in sheep shit and old bones.

38

A year ago, a disaffected zoo worker left several cages open and unlocked the main gate for the animals to find their way out.

An ostrich outran its captors, striding along at a steady thirty kilometres per hour, amazing to watch on television until, eventually, the television crew caught up to it in a shopping mall.

This newly won freedom did not intoxicate all the animals. The ponies—as they appeared on television—looked frightened and anxious. They seemed to know they were where they shouldn't be. Their escape lacked conviction. They were the first to be recaptured, lingering outside the zoo gates. A chimp by the name of Bess was returned to the zoo wearing a woman's slip thought to have been pinched off a clothesline. Pheasants, of all things, were the ones found the farthest away. Flamingos hopped and stepped quickly to the square, where they grouped around the fountain. They looked interested in flight, but also unsure of what to do.

This is the first time I have visited the zoo with both Katie and her mother. Dawn's head turns at every screech. She isn't used to it.

She wonders if Doctor might find the going a bit tough on the outside.

I remind her that he is very adaptable.

Yes, but I wonder if he knows where he is. Where will he go? Will he eventually return to us?

It is a relief to stop at the rhino enclosure. The rhino is as it was last time, still burdened with its heavy coats, head shaped like a boot, as it stands side-on to us. Some pink, and a bit of white in its eye. Like a big woman looking sourly into a shop window.

I don't understand, she says, why he didn't take the younger one with him?

I remind her of the ponies. Perhaps Mole lost his nerve.

I am not enjoying this conversation with Dawn. A prickly heat is coming off me. It's as if I am wearing another layer of clothing. Soon, Dawn will find a thread to pull and very quickly my pretence of ignorance will unravel. She will wonder why I didn't intervene. Why I didn't tell my uncle or the Trustees. She will think me a collaborator. I don't like to think of myself in that way, but, to my surprise, that is what I have become.

Now Katie pipes up to ask why the ape is looking at her like that?

I have no idea, except to say, Why not? She is too young to think of herself as a captor or master of another.

When I first went to the zoo as a boy, I felt superior to all the birds and animals I saw, partly, I think, because I thought of them as unclothed. They looked like the beasts in my child-hood books. Signs everywhere warned people not to get too close. There were cages. Bars. But I was constantly pulled away or held by Mum and Dad—danger was everywhere.

Over at the elephants, Dawn stops to smile. She is back

behind the eye of childhood gazing up at their solid sides. How huge they are, how preposterously large and laboured as they kneel down for the keepers to sweep the dirt off their flanks with yard brooms. A keeper has to place his hands low on the broom for extra purchase, and as the dirt spills the hide appears to move. The troubled eye of the elephant becomes a feeling eye and all feeling shifts to the edges of its face—like someone at the hairdressers intensely aware of the action at the nape of their neck.

The sun catches Dawn's teeth. There is a fine line above her top lip that I have never noticed before. Otherwise, that strain of preoccupation she used to drag through the hotel has left her face.

When Katie runs ahead, Dawn says she told my uncle she would not be returning to the hotel until he released the stranger.

We are staying at my brother's, she says. Did he say?

Yes, he did. Of course he did. The pause is for me to say something more.

He's a stubborn man, your uncle.

We walk on, Dawn with the smiling sadness of someone recently widowed. Her mind turns to the woman in the hat. Is it possible she came for Doctor in the night, and got him out?

How? I ask.

Yes. I suppose so, she says. And then you'd have to wonder why the woman in the hat would leave the younger one behind?

We are back to that.

Ponies, I remind her.

Yes. Yes, she says. But, still.

And don't forget, the stranger did urinate on poor Doctor.

Oh yes, she says. My God, yes. There is that.

We circle back in the puddling rain to where the rhino has worn its trench. It must walk, but every step delivers it to a place it cannot escape from. It must be hard for a rhino to know what to be more distrustful of—the fragility of the ground underfoot or its own enormous weight.

When at last we part at the zoo gates, I feel a tremendous sense of relief. I am alone. There will be no more scrutiny, until next time.

39

I begin each day by opening the doors of all the guestrooms. I leave them like that, just in case. Then, before dinner I close them again.

It is important to keep faith. Uncle Warwick says it is not unusual for hotels to fall out of favour and, sometimes, through no fault of their own, go through hard times. The bad weather, he says, will soon pass.

But it is like living inside an abandoned life. The air has gone out of it. The stairs down to my room have fallen silent. Half the time I find myself addressing a world that is no longer there. Upstairs the atmosphere is more combative. Fumes from the last days of argument between Warwick and Dawn linger. The dining room feels forgotten. In the guestrooms the air is dead.

My uncle's nightly calls to Dawn at her brother's house are torn, and strained. His conversation dries up. Dawn cannot see his port-coloured face, cannot see how deeply grievance has lodged in him. A wildness in his eye. A softness everywhere else. After he hangs up he sits a while scratching his chin. As always, their talk concerns the fate of the stranger—Mole—and the emptiness of the hotel. Dawn cannot get him to see how the two things are bound up. Warwick doesn't want to hear it.

At times, I believe he would prefer it if Mole were dead or that he disappear into the mist, like the legendary Doctor.

My uncle has that fat man's confidence. It is not easy for him to change course. But whenever he speaks of things improving he sounds like one of those tired tennis coaches encouraging the midweek ladies to hit the next ball better.

At dinner he reaches for the salt shaker, then puts it back. He's not hungry. I try to get him to talk, about anything. But if I ramble on too long, his glance falls into empty space. The scraping of the soup spoon is suddenly too loud. The cutlery on the plates makes a ringing lonely sound. When Viktor offers the wine bottle, Warwick doesn't turn it down.

He feels abandoned—by the Trustees, by Dawn. The first little headwind and they're off, he says. I don't mind telling you, Sport, I am disappointed. But you're here. Viktor's here.

For weeks now, we have been stuck with leaden skies. A break in the cloud fills with a blue radiance and the promise of something new.

That is what he hopes for when I come inside. It is exhausting to be the bearer of bad news.

Is there any word? asks the stranger. He means the woman in the hat. Have I heard anything?

This morning I hesitated. I felt a shocking temptation to lie. No, I said.

Inside after feeding out, I enter the lobby and my uncle's look of expectation is like the stranger's. Again a lie rushes to be spoken.

More bad news this evening. A large booking had cheered

my uncle into thinking the tide was turning, but now they'd rung to cancel. He'd already sent me across the road for more supplies. Together we'd spent an hour polishing the banister and vacuuming three rooms. He was fixing up the dining room when I came in to tell him.

Why? he asked.

Something had come up they said.

It was the worst excuse, not quite a lie but in that company. Warwick kicked at the air in front of the piano and lost his balance. As he recovered it, he must have seen my father smiling up at him because he picked up the photo and hurled it against the wall. The glass in the frame shattered surprisingly easily. The picture of my parents fluttered and drifted to the floor. My uncle walked across and stood over the broken glass and photo. He looked up, sad and shocked, like a big kid dismayed at himself.

Sport, I'm really sorry. I'll get a new frame tomorrow.

And I want it back, I said.

Yes. Of course, he said. Of course.

I left him there—staring down at the mess he'd made—and went to do the feeding out.

The stranger was at the mesh waiting for me.

I heard a noise, he said.

I passed his bowl through the feeding hole—pasta, with pesto, some chopped parsley, a bit of parmesan. The stranger eats what we do these days.

I heard a noise, repeated the stranger.

Yes, I said. My uncle threw a photo of my parents against a wall.

The stranger nodded and looked down at the bowl in his hands.

What will you do? he asked. He looked at me carefully, held his head on one side.

I felt *looked at*. That old complaint. As if there was something wrong with me that he could see and I was still to find out.

The next afternoon, I answered a knock on my door to find Viktor out of his chef's pants and grimy white jacket. His new shoes got my attention. An ironed shirt collar poked out from a smart charcoal coat that, like the shoes, was a surprise.

He'd come to say goodbye. He'd taken a job in another town, in a restaurant, a proper one, he said.

Viktor was already halfway out the door. I could feel it in his handshake; see it in his eye. I was no longer his boss's nephew. I was just a colleague to say goodbye to. I felt bad that until now, on the day of his departure, he'd chosen to keep his new job a secret from me. I'd felt the same when Dawn moved out. I'd wondered what else I had missed.

What about the stranger? I say. Have you said goodbye to him?

Viktor backed into the cold light of the stairwell, and looked away.

It is cold in the backyard, but there's still some heat rising off the pen. That's the good thing about building with stone.

Only the mesh area around the gate and feeding hole has been left unclad. The wall facing the basement window blocks out the light, which, from the stranger's point of view, is a loss, but from my point of view is a blessing. Days can go by when, apart from feeding out times, I almost forget he is there.

At night it is a different story, of course. The screaming. There is no end to it. And now Viktor is going, no doubt it will be up to me to find a way to silence him. I couldn't bear to pick up the hose.

The stones offer more dignity—a point I made to the Trust in one of its last meetings. The stones provide a greater sense of domesticity and homely pride.

Viktor picks up a small stone to tap against the wall. We wait for the stranger to call out 'yes' before we carry on around to the open side.

He is sitting on the log ready to receive us in front of his impressive winter garden. The moment he sees Viktor with his bag, he gets to his feet.

I'm going, Viktor tells him. More brightly he adds, I have a new job.

The stranger looks unimpressed, as if bigger news is still on its way. It's a shame Doctor is no longer with us. He'd have known what to say. Offered some congratulations.

Instead it's left to Viktor fill in the awkwardness.

I'm going this afternoon, he says. There's a bus.

Still no response. Other than the toe of the stranger's boot scratching in the dirt.

Did you hear what Viktor just told you?

Who will feed me? he asks.

On our way up the stairs Viktor's face is clenched. The scrambled eggs and chopped chives and parsley were my idea, not Dawn's, and I had to fight your uncle all the way on it, he says.

I didn't know that. I tell Viktor I will make sure the stranger knows.

It is only four o'clock in the afternoon, but in the lobby it feels much later. The last globe in the chandelier has gone out—easily fixed, but Uncle Warwick has done nothing about it.

Viktor pauses at the door, and looks back.

I should say something to your uncle, he says.

He knows you're leaving?

Yes.

Well, if there's more to say, you can write to him.

Yes, that's better. That's what I'll do, he says.

I take the bag from his hand. I want to carry it for him. I'm quite happy to walk him to the bus station. Someone needs to see him off.

This is the first time I have seen Viktor outside the hotel grounds. At the end of the drive, he looks back fondly. There is a pull in his eye. He draws a big breath, then turns away, and off we go.

You could come too, he says.

I laugh.

No, really, he says.

I have to remind him. Who would take care of the stranger?

Viktor nods, and we walk on. His stride is longer than I am used to. Out in the street his eyes lift. There is excitement in his cheeks.

At the station, buses are moving sluggishly in and out. A slow shuffle of purpose, lines of bored faces in their windows as they bounce across the gutter out into the world.

I wait for Viktor's face to appear in a window. We wave, and his face slides down the road.

The town feels emptier than usual. There is little traffic. I can even hear the river burbling along at the bottom of the hill. Down the street the lights are on in Mr Byrd's bookshop.

I look the other way as I pass. I walk past the high brick warehouses, empty and boarded up. They hold a memory of this town that few remember. The streetlights end and I walk on in the dark. I know where I am. This is the way the strangers came. The other side of the road is edged with trees. Through their branches I can hear the slap of the river. A light breeze pushes from behind.

I have half an idea to look for the truck. I walk to the edge of town and wait to see what happens.

But the road is in the shadow of the hill. If the truck comes by, will I be seen in the dark? The sunny bend is several hundred metres up the road. I set off in its direction.

A few cars pass. But no trucks. If I keep walking perhaps one will come. For the first time in a long while it feels as if I am doing something. I am thinking for myself. I am getting away at last.

40

The first stars are out. I've never known how to read the sky. The empty paddocks feel like they are waiting for someone other than me.

I walk on. One hour. Two hours. I am wearing Dad's mustard corduroy jacket. A hat and a scarf would be useful. About now my uncle will be thumping down the stairs to look for me. He will have to go out to the backyard to ask the stranger if he knows my whereabouts. There is no one else to ask.

I used to wonder if the strangers had developed special night vision. I don't recall them ever bumping into one another or falling over the log. But I can see perfectly. Partly because I find what I expect to. The hillsides grow more visible. On the rise I see the silhouette of a large steer. As it lifts its enormous head it erases a white moon. In the other direction, a sheep yard filled with groaning sheep. I hurry past the lights of a farmhouse.

I walk on for another hour, then at the end of a drive I rest on a wooden milk delivery stand. Hardly any traffic has come by. I am still waiting for the truck when a pair of headlights sweep around a bend and light the road at my feet. I lean back into the shadow of a tree, and the car passes.

There had been plenty of times when the strangers paced right through the night—as if they had had a destination.

Our farmhouse is twenty-seven kilometres from town. I figure I have walked nine or ten kilometres already.

The road begins to climb and circle the night. Behind me sits the glittering edge of town. After another twenty-five minutes I stop where I thought the car had left the road. It is too dark to see anything. I try listening like I used to, at night, to the strangers' whisper. I don't hear anything. A lonely owl. And I walk on.

I would think it was about ten o'clock when I arrived at the farm. The lights were on. New people were in there. I didn't know much about them. A family, I believe, but I'd been told at a time when I didn't want to hear that my old life was over.

I climbed over the gate in case the clank of chain alerted the dogs. The gravel on the drive was loud, so I moved onto the grass. It hadn't been mown for a while and was wet with dew. I could hear the television as I stepped lightly onto the verandah.

A couple sat on the couch, the woman at one end, the man with his arms spread. Both looked up when a girl in a school uniform came into the room. She handed an exercise book to her mother. The man's attention returned to the television. Indians on war ponies were fanned out along the ridge. Our television had been smaller and had stood in the other corner. The walls had been painted. New curtains hung stiffly either side of the window. Some work must have been done to the fireplace. A fire was roaring, but there was no smoke.

The mother stood up with the exercise book in hand and

left the room with her daughter.

I walked around to the other side of the house. The kitchen window cast light onto the grass. I noticed a smaller child's clothes on the washing line.

Mother and daughter sat at a big wooden table, the exercise book open before them. A small boy in pyjamas appeared in the doorway and wiped a hand across his eyes. The woman at the table got up and led him back into the hall.

I was looking at a vase of lavender on the sill above the sink and did not see the girl get up—until her face appeared near mine. She looked straight at me. And my heart heaved. Two eyes, still and clear as she ran the tap to fill a glass of water. She wasn't looking to see out. She was thinking about something, perhaps her homework. As she raised the glass to her mouth, she kept her hand on the tap. Something I used to do at that tap. But it was her hand, not mine. She looked completely at home. She left the kitchen. The door into the hall was open. The hallway floor had been sanded. The boards gleamed under the ceiling light. The wallpaper had been replaced with a kind of antique yellow maize colour.

I walked around to the side of the house and stopped at the window of Mum's sewing room. There was enough light from the hall to see my old bed parked in there. It looked narrow and meanly thin, and I felt a fondness for my bed back at the hotel. Unexpectedly we had grown into one another.

At the north end of the house I found the banana tree. It was now a stump.

As I ran back to the road I expected the dogs to start up. But there wasn't a single bark.

What had I hoped for? I had let an idea—a fantasy—get hold

of me. At the time I didn't question it, but went along thinking it would deliver me to somewhere familiar. But that place had gone.

And now? I was tired. The thought of walking all the way back tired me more.

Some kilometres on, I climbed over a farm fence. At one end of the paddock a tree cast a generous amount of shadow in the moonlight. I ducked under the low branches and got as close to the trunk as I could. I scuffed away pellets of old sheep shit and lay down. The stars held firm through the branches, but I could not. The tree's roots broke the surface and it was like lying on bones. I turned over and lay there, until my ribs got sore, then I changed position again. This time I rolled into a ball. And when that didn't work I sat up with my back to the trunk and drew my knees up as I had seen the strangers do.

My efforts to get to sleep made me fretful. I stood up and ducked under a branch to piss. The air froze around me and I hurried back to where I had lain.

Eventually the desire to sleep passed out of my hands.

I woke some time later on my side and on top of the corduroy jacket. I couldn't remember taking it off. One side of me felt bruised. But, oddly, I didn't feel cold. I burrowed back down to see if I could get some more sleep. But it was hopeless. It was as if my body had had a change of mind because now it was too cold to be still.

I left the tree and climbed back over the fence to the road. I would have thought I'd be hungry. I walked on feeling springy in myself.

I was a good way along the road when the hills began to push out of the dark. Patches of green shadows came into view.

Sheep, still dazed by the night, began to move.

A little after the sun lit up the road a sparkling red van stopped to ask if I needed a lift.

About an hour after that, Uncle Warwick's car snuck over a raised section of road.

The car slowed, and crept the last thirty metres until it drew level with me. The window wound down. Uncle Warwick removed his sunglasses. He held them up to the mirror, then rubbed their lenses on his shirt. Then he looked across at me, and smiled. Hello, Sport, he said.

41

Each morning I boil the stranger his egg. Two eggs if there are enough. I take him morning tea. Sandwiches at lunch. I make sure he gets whatever Uncle Warwick and I have for dinner. The stranger is noticeably perkier. It also helps that some warmth has returned to the sun.

The still days are stunning, each one a miracle stolen from the loosening grip of winter. And if that weren't enough, the stranger must be encouraged too by the tall silverbeet, and the sprouted carrots.

This afternoon Uncle Warwick came down to the backyard on one of his rare visits. The significance did not escape the stranger—he rose up from the log, one hand on his left knee, then he straightened.

His whiskers have grown darker and wilder over the winter; they make his eyes seem brighter, more alert.

He looked with interest at the tennis racquet in my uncle's hand.

Closer to the cage, Warwick's eyes began to water. He doubled over, gagged, and spat on the path. He waved his hand for the hose. Changed his mind and unscrewed it from the tap. He stuck his mouth under the nozzle and ran the tap.

Christ, he said. Christ. He threw his head back and gargled, then handed me the end of the hose to reattach.

Water dripping off his chin, Uncle Warwick took a tennis ball from his pocket.

Do you think he would like a ball?

Ask, I say.

My uncle held out the ball as the stranger approached the feeding hole.

He won't bite? he laughed.

I laughed too, but it didn't make his fear go away.

The stranger accepted the ball, and turned it over in his hands to examine it.

I wished he'd had the grace to say thank you. It's not hard to do, and it would have prevented the frown spreading across Uncle Warwick's face. It might be a small thing, but it is what agreeableness depends upon.

It's yours if you want it, Warwick told the stranger. Something to occupy yourself with. You can throw it against the stones. Or you can just throw it up in the air and catch it.

The stranger's lips moved. Barely a whisper.

Thank you, he said. The ball is an unexpected gift.

We have a guest! But that jubilation passed quickly. The guest has a problem with the window. It won't close properly. It is stuck. The guest stooped in front of the window to make his point. Cold air swept in under the sash.

I am more interested in the strangers' occupancy of the room which it seemed to remember as if it were just yesterday. Doctor, or the older stranger as we knew him in those days, lying back on his pillow, eyes closed, hands folded on his chest like a dead pope. The younger whippet on the mattress, staring up at the ceiling with a frosted apprehension, which in hindsight seems to have been a glimpse into the future.

The stranger has gained weight. It is quite noticeable in his face but also in the heavier way he gets up from the log these days, dropping a hand onto his thigh to push himself up, reminiscent of Doctor.

The woman in the hat, he begins. I believe she was here last night?

There is still a look of wonder about him as he pushes forward. Then his face is intercepted by the mesh.

There, in the backyard, I was sure I heard her. Did you see her? The woman in the hat?

I fork some pasta through the feeding hole, but the stranger stays put. I don't know what to tell him. The woman in the hat has been in our lives for as long as the strangers have. I don't know if she is real or not.

The tennis ball is clutched in his hand. He looks at it in a companionable way, as if seeking its opinion, then glances up at the hotel windows.

It's been some time since I saw a light come on, he says.

Business has been quiet.

I think I last saw a light on in winter, he says.

Yes. That's possible.

There are no guests, he says, and he waits for me to explain.

But I can't. Nor can Uncle Warwick. If we could, we would find a way to attract them back, and a whole line of loyal guests would file through the front door with amazing stories about being lost at sea.

And the Trustees he says. I have not seen any of them for quite some time.

The Trust has been wound up, I tell him, glad at last of some news to pass on.

Why was I not informed? he asks.

What can I say? That Doctor's disappearance had spooked them? Along with some of the more negative comments received in the complaints box. Or that people aren't so interested in him anymore. They have turned their attention back to saving for retirement, fixing their teeth.

The girl? asks the stranger.

On holiday, I reply.

And her mother?

Gone with her.

Lie upon lie. They stack up.

Now the stranger is looking at me, as if he hopes to find in me something new.

You know, he says. I once played tennis.

But that's all he says. That's all the opportunity I give him. The pasta is getting cold.

His mouth opens wide and I poke the fork in above a line of unbrushed teeth. His pink tongue looks healthy enough.

And here is another thing I would have loved to report to the Trustees—the stranger hasn't come down with a single cold or a sore throat over the winter. It really is amazing.

At last, the days are drawing out. Across the road Mr Hughes in stunning white shirt sleeves is putting his fruit out on display. The pavement around his feet blazes in sunshine.

At the zoo, the trees are budding. They have a greater

impact on Dawn than on me. In their transformation there is something to look forward to.

We continue to meet there.

She and Uncle Warwick speak on the phone. But that's it. She says she's made it clear that she won't return to the hotel until the stranger is set free. There is nothing more to be gained from the stranger's captivity. If he had anything to say we would know by now. So what is the point?

I have asked my uncle the same question. Letting him out would mean giving in, but my uncle cannot do that.

We stop by the fake mountain home of the ibex. Two animals standing on hind legs butt each other. Then, as their forelegs land, they turn away, suddenly uninterested, as though what just happened was instinct, nothing more, and its pointlessness had struck them at exactly the same moment.

We wander on. A distant roar. Something squeals overhead.

Is he eating properly?

Uncle Warwick?

Yes. Sausage. Pasta.

Greens?

From the stranger's garden.

It's one of those transactions that provides all parties with a degree of dignity and satisfaction—the stranger because he can barter a bunch of silverbeet for an hour or two longer on the plate warmer. Or a snack from the bar. Although I've noted to Uncle Warwick that that resource is running low.

The other day Warwick asked me if I had washed the silverbeet.

Of course, I said.

I mean really washed it, he said, and with an aggrieved look he identified a speck of soil that looked as though it could have come from the stranger's ablutions area. In my effort to persuade him that any traces of soil had come from the vegetable garden, I found myself siding with the stranger. Why, I asked Warwick, would the stranger do that?

But I see no reason to tell this to Dawn.

At the zoo, everything is shitting. Birds shit from their perches. The ibex flexes its anus and expels little balls of black shit. There is little left to the imagination. There is not much the ibex may keep to itself, except for the big matter of what it is to be an ibex.

And the stranger? she asks.

I think he is coping.

The clear nights have been cold lately.

I remind her that I did build him a stone shelter, and every night I turn on the plate warmer.

I bet Warwick complains, she says.

I don't think he minds at all.

You mean he doesn't care? Really?

I tell her the stranger has been having night visions. The woman in the hat, I say. He's convinced she showed up the other night in the backyard.

And did anyone else see this woman in a hat?

Can anyone see another's vision? I ask, and Dawn changes the subject.

Katie is back at school. She misses her dad. They speak every night, and sometimes he picks her up from the school gate and drops her off at Dawn's brother's.

She misses you, too, says Dawn.

We stop at an enclosure and a sweeping shadow startles us.

A forest eagle, with two mice in its beak, lands on a stump. It shoves one mouse under its claw and juggles the other in its beak, juggling and juggling. Then down it goes, the mouse, until only its tail and back legs are visible. The eagle gobbles again, the white mouse shifts. There is just the tail to go. Then it is gone.

I run all the way back to the hotel, run until I am out of breath. What a strange moment for Dawn to return to the subject of Doctor's disappearance.

42

Now that the sun has fully returned to the backyard, the grass has taken off. I've mown it twice in the past fortnight. The stranger asked for the clippings to cover the filth inside his pen.

I had a chat to Uncle Warwick about it. He couldn't think of a reason why not.

It was probably less than hygienically ideal as I had to pass the clippings through the feeding hole. And I had to wear sunglasses. These days the glare from the stones is fierce. Not to mention the stench—in warm air it is more challenging.

At the zoo I told Dawn it was Uncle Warwick's idea to dismantle the stone walls, to let in more light and to improve the stranger's living conditions.

Dawn had to stop. Warwick thought of that? she asked.

He has given the stranger a ball to play with, as well, I said.

Good Lord, she said. And the stones, what is to be done with them?

We will build a new wall, I said.

The stones reek of the cold and damp, but lifting them is a bit like raking away old leaves. The smell of low-lit afternoons departed with the stones. Sunlight landed on the floor of the pen. Within a few days of steady sunshine the soil inside the cage was hard enough for the stranger to bounce his ball. The ball takes him all over the cage. And now his footprints are everywhere.

I get out there first thing, often before the stranger has woken. It's quite something to witness. The way he uncurls and brings his hands up above his head and stretches has a lengthening effect on his legs. One hand has a grip of the tennis ball. His mouth spreads into a yawn. His eyes open to find my face above the wall witnessing his slow awakening from winter recess. He blinks in the bold new light. I smile at his confusion and get back to work.

The work is easier this time around and, unexpectedly, more satisfying—I feel like I am dismantling winter and installing summer.

I also have the feeling the stranger will be prepared to pitch in and help if it speeds up the change of season.

On his feet, his eyes squinted, he had to turn away from the sun. I gave him my sunglasses.

Imagine an ape with sunglasses on, I said to Dawn.

She began to laugh, then stopped herself.

No, she said. I refuse to think of him in that way.

The smell, though, is terrible. Uncle Warwick has had to buy me a surgical mask to protect my airways.

After a week of solid work the old mesh sides of the cage were exposed—they looked like old fishing net warped by the sun. The stone lay in piles.

Joe Phillips turned up with the portable holding pen, then with Stein the two of them drafted the stranger into it, so I could work unhindered inside the cage.

I set to work with a rake. I didn't enjoy working over Doctor's grave. I could not forget it was there. I was happier later walking up and down the cage casting grass seed from a bag.

Out of nowhere another one of those early spring fronts clipped the town, and we rushed indoors to escape the rain. In the kitchen we sat around drinking tea and eating cake.

A few hours later the sky broke to stunning sunshine, and we returned outside. The downpour had done little damage to the newly sowed area. There were some puddles, but it was pleasing to see how quickly they drained away.

The stranger sat in the holding pen soaking wet. His dripping beard dragged his mouth open. He sat so still it was as if he were willing himself to dry. After the steady rain the sun surprised us. It was hotter than it had been for months. Uncle Warwick had to dash inside for his hat.

Now that I have started on the new wall, I look for stones to fit snugly together while wedging smaller ones into a cushion of wet mortar.

When he came out to check on my progress, Uncle Warwick wore a surgical mask. I told him I needed a concrete mixer and his interest wandered across to the creature inside the holding pen.

The next morning Uncle Warwick tied a rope around the stranger's waist and double-knotted the other end to the mixer. I explained the cement, sand and water ratio to the stranger, and we went to work.

I think he relished the open air. It is quite pleasant work— repetitive, but satisfying to be part of a joint effort. The stranger stopped when I did. We had a cup of tea on the porch. With him out of the cage, I was more aware of his smell. I had to gulp down the dregs at the bottom of my cup.

The wall will have a thickness of four stones. But how high should it be?

Warwick ran inside to get his tennis racquet. He played a few casual shots. After the balls sprayed around the yard, I reassured him that the wall would have a smooth finish. I also argued for extra height to intercept the occasional errant shot.

The stranger, trailing the rope from his waist, listened and nodded.

When I look down from the toilet window I am struck by the wall's partitioning effect. The grass inside the cage looks painted on. The backyard now holds two worlds. Neither is aware of the other. My uncle bangs away on one side with his racquet and ball. The stranger squats and shits on the other.

But does it keeps the wind out? asks Dawn. You know what it is like at this time of year with the equinox gales.

It is much better than before. Remember when the wind and the rain tore through there in the storm?

She looks away.

She must remember, surely?

She does. But she doesn't like to.

The flamingos delay us but fail to hold us. We wander on until we arrive back at the elephant enclosure. I have to work hard to get Dawn's attention. The elephant is languid. It is like watching a great body of sand find movement within itself.

I have something else to share with Dawn. Yesterday, after Uncle Warwick mishit a volley, the ball had to be retrieved from the other side of the wall. There was the usual blinding effect as we left sunny Wimbledon to encounter the cage's filthy inhabitant. There must be a hole somewhere in the roof because the stranger greeted us with Uncle Warwick's ball in his hand. Then, without any instruction he passed it through the feeding hole.

I would like to hit a tennis ball, the stranger said. It has been years since I last did and, with the warmer weather upon us, it would lift my spirits if I could be let out to play.

Uncle Warwick's mind seemed to circle around that possibility.

No, he said. No. I don't think so.

Can he even play tennis? asks Dawn.

He claims to. But people will say anything to persuade another of their credentials.

And Doctor?

Still, no word.

The ibex are out in number today. Their fur is matted and dreary. As there is no rain, their misery must come from within.

And what about your uncle? How is he faring? Is he happy?

I cannot reliably say. At times he looks like a man who has lost everything and is blindly following his days for want of any alternative comfort. We continue to play tennis. On court, at least, some of his old desire is revealed.

We carry on to the zoo cafe. Usually we don't stop. The coffee is bad and the service is surly. But Dawn wants to sit. Too much has drifted by. She wants the roars and squawks to come to her. We watch the people at the next table bite into their stale baguettes.

Conversation returns to the practice wall. She says she can't imagine it. She cannot place it in the backyard she knew.

Describe it for me, she says.

From the upstairs toilet window the view of the segregated backyard can be confusing. I find I can concentrate on one side or the other, but not both at the same time. There is the stranger, like a man sitting under a palm tree alone on his island, and there is my uncle monotonously hitting a tennis ball. Where else in the world would you find such a scene? I would not know what to call that place. Although, at the zoo, where, from their fake mountain aspect, the ibex look into the elephant world even though in their alpine homeland there are no elephants.

And what about you, dear boy? she asks. What do you do all day?

I have my own schedule. That is what I cling to. Feeding out, and construction work lately. And if I am not too tired— the clarinet. That is what makes me reliably present—my schedule. That is what it comes down to.

She does not ask me if I am happy. Or if I have met anyone special. Or if I have come up with a plan for myself. I wonder if she knows about the night spent at the farmhouse. Surely she would say something if she knew. I feel I should be more discreet when I talk about Warwick. I shouldn't really have told Dawn about him wearing the same shirt for days on end. Or that he hardly ever changes his slippers for shoes.

We leave our undrinkable coffee. By the flamingos Dawn stops to gaze up at the gathering cloud.

I have never known it to rain as much as it has this spring, she says.

And, just like that, she is in the backyard, as it used to be, with the strangers in a huddle, or scampering from one side of the cage to the other.

We walk on—and talk turns to the woman in the hat. Who is she? How on earth did the strangers came up with such a person? Or did we—the Trust? It would be fair to say the woman in the hat now has a greater presence in the stranger's life than Doctor.

Is this the moment to unburden myself and speak of Doctor's miserable end?

But Dawn cries out 'Look!' She is delighted as an elephant sweeps acorns into a pile—and reaches up with its trunk to place the bounty in its toothless mouth.

Uncle Warwick's a lot thinner since he stopped drinking, I say.

She is amazed. Not even one glass at dinner?

No.

Does he miss me? she asks.

Of course he does, I tell her.

My uncle is quieter these days, more agreeable. I wonder if that is worth mentioning? Or that he replaced the broken photo frame, and made a point of delivering it to my door. I decide it's not. I would have to tell her how it broke.

Dawn leaned nearer and whispered into my ear. Has Warwick said anything?

About what?

She smiled.

In that case, it'll be a surprise.

I can't remember the last time I saw the stranger doing press-ups—it must be months ago—but that's what he was doing when I got back to the hotel.

And Warwick, he was in a strangely upbeat mood. The doors and windows were open. He hurried about the place, whistling.

I was a bit late with feeding out. The stranger didn't complain. The thrill of fish was in his mouth.

He was careful at first, as though he couldn't quite believe he was eating fresh fish, but then he ate quickly, wanting to get to the next forkful, and the next one and the next one.

Then he stopped, his mouth went slack. There were bits of mashed fish on his tongue and stuck to his lip.

I turned to look behind, then I saw her too—coming around the end of the wall—the woman in a hat.

43

Dense pine climbed from the valley floor to the lit ridge. The trees—dark towards their roots and sunny at their tops—gave the impression of floating. A single cloud grew white and the sky around it turned a deep blue. And the last of the rooftops pushed up into the new day. The valley spread before us, and we drove on.

Look, said Joe Phillips. It's not a big deal. What about stray cats? People bring cats out here all the time when they tire of them.

Grassland rolled away on both sides of the road. We met up with the river and left it behind. The road straightened and aimed south. We didn't pass another car. From the edge of a worked paddock a man on a tractor waved.

We drove for another two hours, then, at a place of Joe's choosing we pulled over and got out of the truck.

I stayed on the side of the road while Joe climbed onto the tray to unlock the holding pen.

Stein was first to rush out. His front paws slid and stopped him at the edge of the tray.

The stranger, on all fours, followed. Two moist eyes lifted above a tangle of beard towards the purple haze sitting over where we'd come from. My God, it was beautiful. Our lives were stuck in that gorgeous light. It was a surprise to think of the hotel as also being part of it.

Joe gave the stranger a pat on the backside to get him going.

When the stranger showed reluctance Joe yelled, 'Stein!' and the dog jumped off the truck. On the road the dog turned in a tight circle, then barked.

We waited for the stranger to take Stein's lead.

Even out here, in the wide open countryside, he stank. The smell of the cage stuck to him. And, as distant as we were from town, his smell was a reminder that we had not travelled all that far, not as far as we would have liked.

The stranger still wore the same clothes he had when he arrived at the hotel. Rags, as they were now, pressed against him like an extra layer of skin, and with markings that had turned wild.

Joe glanced at his watch. Then he spoke firmly. Come on fella, down you get. Let's get you on your way.

The stranger remained frozen, on all fours.

I remembered the bag of nuts Dawn had given me for the trip. I fetched it from the cab. Broken cashews, chipped Brazil nuts, almonds, salt. I filled the palm of my hand and held the nuts out to him.

The stranger stared suspiciously. Then he chose one. A cashew.

There you go, said the farmhand, as the stranger began to move. The dog crouched low, willing the stranger to make a mistake.

The stranger pushed off with his shoulders, sort of butted his head forward, then drifted back. He looked up and I saw what made him resist. The sky and the horizon were too big a space for him to move his body into. He shifted a few inches on his hands. He brought each knee forward and, as the dog had, he peered over the edge down at the road. It looked as far away as tomorrow.

I remembered the ibex—and the meaningless direction in which they set their gaze. Their memory was of the alps.

As the farmhand reached up to offer his hand, I noticed he kept himself outside of the stranger's striking range.

The stranger didn't want his help. He rolled onto his backside and swung his legs around. Joe Phillips held out a pair of catching hands—again, he meant to encourage. The stranger landed on stiff legs, and the dog barked and shook with excitement.

At first the stranger seemed distrustful of his own uprightness. He gripped a hand to the small of his back to urge himself up the last few inches.

The sun struck his weathered face. The same sun made the bare hills glow. Hills that had never seemed of our time but carried over from another period, like the bones of a carcass long melted away.

The dog barked again, but the stranger didn't move.

Joe Phillips moved to his side—to egg him on. It was like trying to get a twig to catch in the current. The stranger's head turned, but that was all. When Joe came up on his other side the stranger seemed more confused.

He turned in the direction of town and the dog raced around to head him off.

Joe Phillips smiled to show he was amused. He shouted an instruction to Stein.

The stranger had to lift his feet clear of the dog's nips. But he got the idea. He came around, his nose now pointed in the direction of those big white hills. Their stillness was unnerving, as always, as if in possession of something we were still to find out for ourselves.

His movement was slow, painful to watch. Every ten paces or so he faltered, then stopped, and held up a hand to press against the air.

Did he say where he was going? asked Joe Phillips.

No.

Then he's got a hell of a way to go before he gets there.

He enjoyed his joke.

Listen, he said, isn't there a cutting up ahead?

We got back in the truck and followed him at idling speed until we had drafted him past the cutting. Then we pulled over.

I need a smoke, said Joe.

On Bill Francis's plane, floating up where no human being could reasonably expect to be, I had felt all the freedom in the world. Then I looked down and saw just the one narrow road running in and out of where we lived, like a cut in the land-scape that eventually closes over. I'd felt a stab of panic. But now, as I got out to stretch my legs, the same road felt solid and dependable.

The stranger walked on.

A hare flattened back on itself was stuck to the road. An outline, one eye. That's all that was left of it.

From the tray the skittering of paws. The dog wanted to leap down but another instinct would not allow it to. Cigarette smoke drifted from the side window. I continued to gaze into

261

country I knew but had never walked. The view settled back to long dry grass bending in the wind and the enormous backs of cattle. All the while the stranger grew smaller and more distant until he was more a part of the road than he had ever been a part of our lives.

AUTHOR'S NOTE

I wish to thank Michael Heyward for his unflagging encouragement, and editor Jane Pearson for her flawless and astute eye.

The startling observation 'There is a peaceful aliveness in dead faces' (page 214) is from Svetlana Alexievich's *Boys in Zinc*, Penguin Modern Classics, 2017.

I also wish to thank the DAAD Artists-in-Berlin Program for granting me a residency in Berlin in 2015–16, where much of *The Cage* was conceived.